32: REFUSE TO LOSE

MIGNON MYKEL

Cover Design and Formatting: oh so novel
Editor: Jenn Wood, All About the Edits
All images have been purchased

PROLOGUE

August 24

"Oh, my God!" Callie's laugh filtered through my lust-filled haze.

...As did the pain radiating up my leg from stubbing my goddamned toe on the bed frame.

I let out a hissing '*fff*' rather than yell out that very word, all while my damn leg threatened to give out from under me. I hit that bastard really fucking hard.

So much for the "lose the clothes and take me now" that came the moment I came through the door, not even five minutes ago.

"Trevor!" My name on her lips came out high-pitched as she pounded on my bare shoulder. My hands tightened under her ass and her arms banded around my neck. "Don't drop me."

My face was pressed to her upper chest and part of me really wanted to focus on those soft, round pillows that were

1

right there, but I was having a really hard time taking my focus off the pain in my foot.

Even my dick was having a hard time keeping itself, well...hard.

It took a lot of mental focus, but I managed to lower Callie to the bed gracefully, only to flatten her to her back as I lay on top of her, my face buried deep in the pillow her head rested on.

"Godfuckingdamn," I mumbled into the feather and cotton.

Callie's hands rested on my lower back and she slowly dragged her nails up my back. "Poor baby."

"This damn bed..."

She laughed again, and when her fingers reached my hair, she tugged until I lifted my head from the pillow.

"Has always had that metal foot. It didn't just jump out and attack your foot." Her smile took over her entire face and shit, if the thought that she was the most beautiful woman I'd ever been with didn't nearly take the pain away.

We'd been together for a little over a year, and I was ready to take us to the next step. After the week we'd just had...

I didn't have a fancy proposal planned, but I did have a pretty fancy ring for her. One that would tell the world she was very much taken, but not so fancy that it would get in the way of her work.

Callie's hand in my hair tugged my face to her and soon her lips were pressed against mine. God, I couldn't wait to know I could do this damn near every day of my life, forever and ever after. As her hands relaxed against my head, I rolled us over so she was sprawled on top of me, her legs out along mine as her feet hooked over my shins.

When I grabbed her ass, kneading the round softness in my hands, Callie sighed into my mouth. I was quickly growing hard again and she pulled up on her knees, not breaking the kiss, as she reached for my cock.

I slipped my hands around her, from her ass up to the other pillowy softness on this beautiful woman I had the pleasure of calling mine. I cradled her breasts in my hands, sweeping my thumbs over the tips as she slowly sank down on me. Our moans were harmonious, but while I kept my eyes open and trained on her face, her eyes closed and she bit the side of her lip.

The moment she was fully seated, I alternately squeezed her nipples, one then the other, again and again quickly until her eyes popped open, showing me the bright blue orbs. They were usually some shade of teal, but when she was turned on, the green overtook and it never failed to shock me.

Letting go of her nipples, I brought one hand to her lower back, the other to her neck, bringing her near as I crunched up enough that I could bring her chest to me, sucking a breast into my mouth.

I suckled on the end of her C-cup beauty, my tongue playing over the rock-hard peak, and her hands were back in my hair, right where I wanted them to be.

Digging my heels into the bed, I lifted my knees enough that I could start rocking up into her, all while Callie ground herself down over me.

"Trevor." My name on her lips was a breathy whisper. She pressed her chest into my face and tightened one of her hands in my hair. The pain-pleasure thing going on was *just right*.

So right.

I pulled my mouth from her breast and lifted my chin as she dropped hers. With this kiss, everything began to move faster.

Mouth to mouth.

Tongue over tongue.

I grabbed her hips and held her still, then quickly began to thrust up into her, my balls tightening with each swing.

Our mouths met one another, move for move, a delicate dance we'd perfected—a dance that was filled with passion.

Everything with Callie, every moment, every thought, was the definition of passionate. Our life, our fights, our love.

And I wouldn't have it any other way.

When her mouth stilled against mine and her breath hiccupped against my mouth, I flipped us again. Her legs automatically wrapped around my hips, her feet crossing at my back. I tore my mouth from hers to press open-mouth kisses to her neck.

"Shit, Cal." I licked her pulse point before biting gently.

"Trev." Her breath hitched. "T-Trevor." Her arms tightened around my neck and soon she was arching into me. We were pressed together, every inch of her to every inch of me.

"Ohmigod." Her legs tightened, and soon I felt her thighs quivering against me. I slowed my thrusts. I needed to last a little longer. I wanted this to go on for a little longer more.

But her clenching walls were my undoing. One firm squeeze of hers—Callie's way of keeping her orgasm going; this wasn't our first rodeo—and I was a fucking goner.

"Shit." I grunted against her neck and no matter how hard I tried to hold my orgasm back, soon I was jetting hot streams into her waiting heat.

My hips jerked against hers and I felt as Callie nuzzled her face into my neck, pushing my own face away from her. Her smile pressed there, right before she gave me four soft, pecking kisses.

As my body calmed, I brought my lips to hers. Our kisses now, were light. Sweet. Comfortable.

Home.

This is what I wanted.

Forever.

I wanted to come home from games, to her. I wanted to love on her throughout the night, only to wake up and do it again.

I wanted to marry her. Give her babies. Watch as her belly filled round with kiddos that were every bit her, with maybe a slight rebellious streak from me. Raise them in a house we picked out together. Watch them stumble through life and make friends, find love, and then cheer on as they went through the same events she and I did.

My buddies all had a hell of a time to get to that point.

Caleb damn near lost Sydney to his stupidity—shithead shouldn't have done the damn dating show to begin with. Jordan Byrd... I still wasn't completely sure why Marlo took his ass back, but they were good again and he was good with their daughter Rori so whatever.

Mikey Leeds...

He'd had a happily ever after. Married the girl of his dreams. Had a kid.

Leeds's hell of a time came after that, in an event that took his wife from him in the form of a car accident. Shit, I could remember the day he got the phone call, while we were out in...hell, I didn't remember. Just that we weren't in San Diego.

Looking at the defenseman, he looked like he was moving along fine but I also knew how hard he'd loved Trina.

I didn't want to go through the struggles my teammates and friends went through. And I sure as hell didn't want something to tear Callie away from me before I could show her I loved her, and that I was going to love her forever.

Something more than the words she finally had the balls to say, seven months ago—well after I admitted them to her.

I didn't ever want to be as stupid as I was this last week.

No more not talking.

No more letting emotions run high.

"Shower?" Callie mumbled into my mouth and I nodded.

She slipped away from me, my softening cock still hard enough to appreciate the pull. Callie was a few feet away before I got with the program and rolled off her bed, following her to the connected bathroom where she was already turning the water on.

I stepped up to her, trailing my hand slowly down her back and, after she stepped into the tub-shower combo, I followed. Standing under the water, Callie reached for my hand, pulling me to her. Soon, we were kissing again.

Slowly, again.

Sweetly, again.

Her hands ran up and down my sides, languidly. I felt as her pinkies brushed over the abdominal cuts on my sides and soon, my cock was twitching again, but I'd hold off.

I ran my hands through her blonde locks, running the water through the ends. The hot water splashed around us, pounding against the tile and ceramic drowning out any other noises.

Callie eventually pulled back, her eyes trained up on mine.

There was something different about her face.

She looked...

Sad.

What?

"What's up, Cal?" I asked, although I was suddenly

afraid of the answer.

The memory of her pouncing on me the moment I walked through door, came rushing back at me. We had excited sex more than once, so it didn't really hit me as odd, especially after the emotional week apart we had, but now...

Callie's eyes flitted between mine and her lips were parted. Her chest was rising and falling noticeably and I knew that if the water weren't on, I'd be able to hear her heavy breaths.

"I accepted the job."

If there were four words that could crush me, it would be those ones.

"You accepted the job."

She pressed her lips together and swallowed hard before nodding.

"B-but..." I paused, trying to control the emotion. I was a fucking fighter on the ice. I didn't stutter.

Callie's chest stopped moving, her eyes locked on mine.

She was holding her breath.

She was taking the New York job. The very one we fought about.

"Really, Cal?" The words left in almost a plea. A breathless plea.

I could feel my world shattering around me.

My heart breaking.

But Callie wasn't saying anything. Instead, her eyes filled with tears.

"God, Cal, give me something here."

Tell me it was a lie. Tell me we could fix this. Fuck, tell me that the assignment wasn't a four-month one, but a four-week one. I could deal with four-weeks.

I didn't get any of those things.

Instead...

"I'm sorry."

7

CHAPTER ONE

March 28
16 months earlier

T<small>REVOR</small>

"YOU DOING ANYTHING SATURDAY?" my captain and best friend, Caleb, asked as we left hockey practice on a Tuesday afternoon. We'd been playing together for the last nine years and both of us should be nearing the end of our careers...but we were still kickin'.

Kickin' ass and taking names.

We had a game tomorrow night and I was looking forward to having the next twenty hours to myself—the one place where I felt my age showed. All the twenty-year-olds were dying to make an impression, hitting the ice at every moment to prove a point, but me? I'd been with the Enforcers for nine years and just resigned another five-year, multi-million-dollar deal.

I wasn't going anywhere. I had nothing to prove. I'd be skipping the optional morning skate tomorrow, instead keeping the company of a five-year-old girl after school, as her mom put together a custom cookie order as part of her company, *sugar&spice*.

A five-year-old girl and her mom, who just happened to be the daughter and ex-wife of an old teammate.

It hadn't been announced yet, but rumor around the locker room was he was coming back to San Diego. Marlo—my friend and the ex-wife—didn't know yet, as far as I knew. Marlo and Jordan's relationship was rocky, at best, and I was prepared for a full shit-storm to hit when he got into town.

So, I had no problem hanging out with those two tomorrow before my pre-game rituals. As for Saturday, it was one of the rare weekend dates we *didn't* have a game and I was planning on taking advantage of it—especially considering that starting next week, we'd be in a rigorous playoff schedule.

"Relaxing. Kicking my feet up. Pounding back a beer or two or ten."

"Why don't you do it at the house? Most of the family will be in town. Ace graduated."

Ace was Caleb's youngest sister, Avery, and she'd been going to school to be a sport agent. No doubt her brothers—there were three of them total—were excited. "Why's she having the party here?"

"No party. Just hanging out at the house." Then, Caleb slapped the back of his hand at my shoulder. "She's in talks with the club. Wants to oversee a few of the players."

"Yeah. You and Jonny."

"I could talk her into taking you on as a client."

"I like my agent." He always had my best interest at hand. When it came time to renew my contract, I didn't want to fight for millions, but I did want to stay with the Enforcers. San Diego, these men...this was home.

I grew up in a backwoods town in the Upper Peninsula of Michigan and while, yeah, it was nice to go home and be with family...

I liked the West coast.

"Yeah, Cord's a good guy. Not like Mark."

I hated to be the pointer-outer of the obvious but, "If it weren't for his ignoring your media clause, you would not have met your wife."

It wasn't intentional, but Mark knew Caleb wasn't the hockey player who wanted to be the face gracing media. But one day, a little redhead domino named Sydney contacted him about a dating show and rather than dealing with it himself—as an agent ought to do—Mark gave her Caleb's direct number.

They met.

And the rest was history.

There was no one for Caleb after meeting Sydney.

According to Caleb though, the only reason why he didn't drop Mark then was because he knew Avery was going to be a great agent and he wanted to support her.

"Besides," I added, "she'll be too fucking busy with Ports." Porter was Caleb's youngest sibling, the baby of the group—and they were a freaking group, the six of them. Porter, like Caleb and Jonny, played professionally but way out in B.F.N.

Okay, okay, for the Charleston Rockets, out in South Carolina.

Still, though, I'd heard horror stories of that kid and the antics he pulled growing up.

We entered the player's garage and the sound of Caleb's truck roaring to life filled the concrete surroundings.

"Dude, it's not even cold out," I said, in response to his remote start.

"Gotta get her warmed up. Her engine likes it." Caleb

winked in my direction and I couldn't help but chuckle, shaking my head.

"Does your wife know you talk like that? That you love your truck more than her?"

"Chief knows she's my number one." Chief was Sydney, not the truck. Not that I would put it past Caleb to name his truck.

"And she knows my mouth and the words that come out of it damn well. Real damn well," he added with a smirk.

"You're a dirty fuck," I chuckled.

Caleb didn't answer, just mmm-ed behind his lips.

Way too much information.

And maybe just enough information that left me envious of the guy. In the nine-plus years I'd known Caleb, he'd been with Sydney for most of them. I teased him once that I had met her first, but he was always quick to come back that if I hadn't flashed her my toothless smile, maybe she would have been interested in me.

Never mind the fact that the only reason why she'd come around was to recruit Caleb for the dating show.

I hadn't stood a chance.

Shit, Caleb really hadn't either, not with how it was supposed to go down, but in the end, it was Sydney he ended up with. She even managed to keep her job as a casting assistant. Now, she was casting all the big shows—and, as much as she grumbled, her best ones were all reality ones.

Hell, I didn't watch much television, let alone reality television, but I made time for the ones my buddy's wife was part of.

In the time I'd known him, Caleb met Sydney, married Sydney, and had her popping out babies left and right. In the beginning, it was funny to watch—Caleb at twenty-five and juggling his first son. Caleb at twenty-seven and his second son.

It was when his daughter was born the following year that the envy started to sink in.

Here I was, in a mix of meaningless relationships—or even relationships that seemed to be going somewhere, only for her to back out—and there he was, having a family and living the life.

"Saturday still stands," Caleb said, breaking away from me as we got to a split in the cars. "See you tomorrow."

BY THE TIME Saturday rolled around, I was itching to get out of my place.

We won both our games during the week—further solidifying our seat in the upcoming playoffs—and after a light practice Saturday morning, I ended up caving and telling Caleb I'd be coming over.

It wasn't the first time I'd been to his place when his entire family was over, but the energy never failed to surprise me. Caleb came from a big family so when I looked at his own brood of four kids, it made sense, but being in the house with his siblings and then his own family...it got loud.

In the driveway of Caleb and Sydney's beachy house was a twelve-passenger van.

I literally laughed out loud when I saw the silver monstrosity. Knowing Caleb's family as I did, I wouldn't put it past his dad to have rented it just for the groan factor.

I parked my truck beside the beast and walked into the house through the garage, a bunch of flowers in hand for Avery, and, after walking through their laundry/mud room, entered the open space that made up the living room and kitchen. Throughout the area, were Caleb, Sydney, and their four kids; Caleb's parents, Ryleigh and Noah, who was essentially the beginning of the Prescott-Enforcers empire; Caleb's oldest sister, Mykaela—who was a hockey legend in her own right, having recently started putting the wheels in motion for a woman's National Hockey Club in the Midwest; Caleb's youngest sister, Avery, the woman of the hour; and Caleb's other sister, McKenna, with her husband and his daughter. Also in attendance, was Caleb's brother, and the Enforcers' goaltender, Jonny, with his wife Jenna, who was talking to some girl I didn't know. I'd been half-expecting to see Porter, too, failing to remember, again, that the kid was old enough to play professionally.

Damn. Knowing Porter was playing pro had a way of making a guy feel old. I met him when he was *thirteen*.

After my small moment of taking everyone in, I walked across the room and handed Avery the bouquet of lilies. "Congrats, kid."

Caleb's baby sister smiled up at me, accepting the flowers. "Thanks, Trev. You know I'm coming after you next, right? My brothers have already agreed to sign once I find a company."

I chuckled at the girl's balls. "And you know I like my agent."

"I'll convince you." Avery nodded, sure of herself—as she should be. She knew the athletic life, the pros and cons of the business, as well as her brothers did. "Give me some time, but I'll convince you."

The thing was—I didn't doubt it.

I looked toward the kitchen to see if Caleb was through with his conversation with Jonny, but it didn't look to be. "Where's your friend?" I asked Avery instead.

"Asher?"

I nodded. I didn't know the logistics of it, but Asher ended up in the Prescott fold at the beginning of the season and what at first seemed to be a few-week thing, turned into something more. The girl had no history, from what Caleb told me, but their mom took her under her wing like a stray kitten.

"In South Carolina."

I lifted my brows, fighting a grin even though part of me was once again kicking myself. "With Porter?" How the hell did the *kid* get a girl, and I was still floundering between relationships?

Avery nodded, smiling. "They're kind of cute."

With that look on her face, I would guess she had a heavy hand in it all. "How much was your doing?"

"This trip, nothing. But maybe a few months ago..." Her voice trailed off as her eyes did the same. Then, she was facing me again, her voice low, to not be overheard. "Jenna brought her sister."

I lowered my voice too, in an exaggerated whisper, as I bent toward her. "I didn't know she had a sister." God, Jenna's parents should have stopped with one kid. Jenna was materialistic. Everything was about show. Money. Whether or not she'd be noticed...

Her parents weren't much different. They weren't exactly the type of people you wanted running the world.

"Caleb wants to set you up."

I frowned, straightening to a stand. "He does not." My voice wasn't lowered this time, and Avery tugged at my arm, bringing me back down.

"Shh! Keep your voice down."

"Ace, Caleb isn't you. Shit, thirty-some-year-old men don't 'set up' their friends at a family get-together."

"Keywords, Trev. Family. Get. To. Gether." She straightened and tilted her blonde head to the side. "Why'd he invite you?"

"Because we're...hockey family." Lame.

"Trust me on this."

I straightened once more and looked back toward the kitchen. Caleb was no longer talking to Jonny and he waved me over, his eyes flashing to his right quickly, where the girl and Jenna were talking.

The girl must be the sister.

She was cute. White-blonde hair pulled into a ponytail. Tiny body. That was the most that I could make out from over here, other than one additional fact. "She's a freaking child," I muttered.

She couldn't be much older than Avery, who just happened to be damn-about ten years younger than me.

Okay, maybe only eight, but fuck.

Jenna's sister was way too young. What the hell was Caleb thinking?

I realized Avery was laughing. "You're really loud."

To prove just that, the girl looked in my direction.

And her cheeks flamed red.

Fuck me.

From across the room, I could see that eyes were a lighter color—I couldn't make out the exact color from here —but I wouldn't be surprised if they were some shade of blue. She looked a lot like Jenna but...

...Sweeter.

If the word could even be applied to a family member of Jenna's.

I turned my back to the girl, trying to get the look of her shock and embarrassment from my mind, and instead face Avery. "I thought we didn't like Jenna," I said, my voice once again low.

It wasn't exactly a secret that Jenna Prescott had very few fans in this room. She was here because she was "family." The Prescotts accepted her well enough, but by her own doing, Jenna distanced herself. The entire time I'd known the Prescotts, Jenna was attached to Jonny, but according to Caleb, Jonny had been a completely different guy before he met, dated, and, eventually, married Jenna.

Avery flattened her hand against my chest, tapping twice with a quick grin. "She's not Jenna."

CHAPTER TWO

CALLIE

I DON'T REALLY KNOW how I got roped into coming to Jenna's in-laws' place.

I knew Jonny's family...*okay*...but I certainly didn't belong at a gathering celebrating the youngest daughter's graduation.

I crossed my arms uncomfortably as I stood in the corner of the kitchen, looking around. Jenna and Jonny—my brother-in-law—just left me standing here. One minute, Jenna was talking to me, and the next, she snapped at Jonny, and they were leaving the room.

I tightened my crossed arms and fought a sigh by puffing out my cheeks. Caleb and Sydney Prescott, the hosts and owners of this very beautiful, yet *modest*—something my sister and brother-in-law didn't know a thing about —home, were pulled apart and talking to different people. I knew Caleb's parents, but they were sitting on the living room floor, playing with their youngest grandkids, Brody— who was one and looked just like his older brothers with

18

dark eyes and bright eyes—and Brielle—who at three, may have been one of the prettiest toddlers I'd ever seen. She had her mom's red hair and a bubbly personality that only little girls managed to encompass.

I turned toward the counter I was leaning on, trying to find something to do.

Shoot, let's be honest, here. Something to *eat*.

I could pass time by eating.

Who the heck knew when Jenna and Jonny would be done doing whatever the heck they were doing, and be willing to take me home. I was supposed to be spending the day with Jenna, planning our parents' thirtieth wedding anniversary. It was the only reason I'd even *gone* to Jenna's.

But my sister literally pushed me back into the elevator of the giant glass building their condo lived in, and said, "We're sending them on a trip to Bora Bora. You owe me five thousand dollars." I'd hardly had the chance to swallow my uprising panic at the dollar signs and she was telling me about going to Jonny's brother's house for something or another.

Essentially, she was holding me hostage.

She knew if I'd been 'set free,' I'd have come up with something else for our parents' anniversary. I knew how Jenna operated. She'd probably just sent off an email to her travel agent when I showed up, and until she knew the plans were in place, she needed me nearby so I couldn't go and derail her plans.

The five-thousand-dollar neon lights flashed in my mind, and I had to fight back the uprising bile.

I didn't even go on vacations for *myself* at that price tag.

Yes, I had a safety net in the bank. But every time it grew over my three-month living budget, I donated it in some fashion—either by direct-check to a charity I believed in, or by finding a mission to fund.

That said, I was currently sitting under my safety net, and five-thousand for an extravagant trip that my parents would no doubt love...

It was going to send me into a panic attack.

I looked down the counter at the food set out. A Prescott party was so unlike a MacTavish one.

Parties at my parents' had champagne fountains and miles of fondue, with caviar and calamari and lobster topping the menu.

There wasn't bacon-wrapped mini-wienies simmering in barbeque sauce, or homemade Chex mix, or cookies that were most definitely decorated by the ten and under crowd.

I uncrossed an arm to reach for one of said cookies, a circle the looked like it'd had a graduation cap piped onto it, that was filled and decorated in the fashion of a certain Brielle Prescott, if the drawings on the fridge were any indication.

But before I could grab it, it was snatched up quickly from under my nose.

I puffed my breath into my upper lip and changed direction, grabbing a plain, undecorated cookie, before looking up at the stealer of the cookie.

I was expecting Caleb's dad. Or even Caleb himself.

He was neither.

Instead, it was the man who had only an hour ago, called me a child.

I gritted my teeth but refused to appear effected by this...this...monstrosity of a man.

My brother-in-law and the men in his family were all tall, easily over six-foot, but this guy wasn't as tall as them. Maybe only five-eleven.

And he wasn't as lean as the others.

His neck was wide, his shoulders bold.

And his forearms...

I swallowed hard—the guy was serious eye candy in the arm department alone—and brought my eyes up to his.

They were gray. Or maybe just a super light blue.

Then he flashed a crooked smile that showed off perfectly straight, perfectly white teeth. The smile pulled the skin taut on his chin, which brought my attention to a thin, puckered line.

A scar.

"You don't look like you're having fun."

Shoot me now. Even his voice was sexy.

Deep and rumbly, like Sam Worthington when he tried to pull off an American accent.

I forced a smile and waved toward him with my cookie. "Being held hostage. I don't really belong."

He bit down on the cookie I was supposed to be eating, as he nodded. "Yeah." He swallowed what was in his mouth. "At least you're family. In a sense."

I was generally a kind person, but his earlier comment wouldn't stop bouncing around in my head. So, with a frown, I decided to ask, "Why are we doing this? I mean, I *am* just a child." Oh, how quickly I found myself on a roll. I put my cookie back down on the counter, untouched, and held up my finger. "For the record, I'm twenty-two. Legal on all fronts."

His eyes dropped down to my waist and traveled back upward, slowly. When his eyes finally met mine again, he had a smirk on his face and maybe a slight redness to his cheeks. "Still too young."

"For what?" I shook my head. "Never mind." I grabbed my cookie and mumbled to myself, "Shit, where's Jenna? Fuck it, I'll just get an Uber." I didn't belong here. I wasn't a Prescott. And for that matter, the Prescotts didn't much care for my sister, which made my being here even more uncomfortable.

"Waitwaitwait." Then his big paw of a hand was on my forearm and I startled. There was an odd sort of *zing* that went through me and I had to fight from jerking my arm back from him.

Instead, I stared at his large, sun-darkened hand on my lighter skin. When his thumb brushed gently along my arm, I sucked in a breath before looking up at him, tightening my lips.

And swallowing hard.

"I'm Trevor." He paused before adding, "Winski."

I didn't say anything.

"And you are...?"

Still, I remained quiet.

He lifted a brow, which revealed another scar on his forehead, this one in an L shape.

"I'm sorry?" he tried again.

Quiet.

"Caleb's sister told me he was trying to set me up with you. It was a knee-jerk reaction. I'm sorry."

It was hard to stay indifferent at that because that was just ludicrous. "He did not." Caleb hardly knew me and it hadn't exactly been Jonny dragging me along to this house party.

"According to Avery..."

His hand on my skin was making me uncomfortable.

Okay, maybe uncomfortable was the wrong word. That energy was still zipping through me and it was unsettling.

Yes.

Unsettling was a better word.

"I'm being held hostage by Jenna," I finally stated, pulling my arm away. The loss of his hand didn't do much for the energy though. Instead, the large span of skin where his hand had been, tingled. I shook my arm discreetly before crossing my arms over my chest.

Once again, curling in on myself, still uncomfortable with being in this home with people who didn't really know me, yet managed to dislike me because they disliked my sister.

I couldn't blame them. I wasn't the biggest fan of my sister all the time either—our parents' anniversary vacation, a prime example—but she was still family. She was still my sister.

"Did you want to leave?" He almost sounded excited by the prospect.

I couldn't help myself. "Children are taught to not go places with strangers."

"I'm not a stranger. I introduced myself. Something you've still failed to do."

I rolled my eyes as I shook my head. "Fine. Callie."

"Well, Callie. Without sounding too forward and rather as an offer to end your hostage situation, can I take you home?"

CHAPTER THREE

TREVOR

SHE AGREED.

I don't know why the hell she did, but she did, and now we were in my truck, traveling southbound on Interstate-805.

Albeit, traveling quietly. Callie hadn't said a word after giving me her address to punch into my Waze app. I glanced at the remaining time; it was going to be a long thirty minutes if there was no talking.

"So, you're Jenna's sister," I broke into the silence.

I was fucking thirty-two—almost thirty-three—years old, and that's how I opened a conversation. I was really hitting it out of the park with this girl.

Callie nodded, glancing at me. "Mmhmm. So, you're Jonny and Caleb's teammate."

I couldn't stop the grin. "Touché."

Her smile was small and tight, and she turned her attention away from me, but I was intrigued.

"Twenty-two, hey?"

Now, her smile pinched tighter.

Mouth, insert foot.

"Shit. Sorry. I mean—"

"Look, whatever you think about Jonny or Caleb trying to set us up, I'm sure it's just a lie. You think I'm a child? Well, dude, you're an old man." She crossed her arms and slide into the corner of her seat and the truck door, angling her body toward me, just a little bit.

I lifted my brows. "I am not an old man."

"I am not a child." Her blonde brows were up and she looked very unimpressed with me.

Why do you care?

I mean, I didn't. She was way too young. She was a fucking MacTavish, too. Materialistic. Opinionated. All about the image.

But this girl...

She didn't come off the same way as Jenna.

Maybe that was why I'd found myself wanting to talk to her at the house; wanting to take her home.

Rescue her from Jenna.

Shit, we all needed a rescue from Jenna, but I was surprised to see her own sister needing it, too.

Where Jenna showed up to the party with dress slacks and a silk blouse, her hair styled—at a salon, I was sure—Callie here was in light-washed jeans with a giant hole in one knee, and a bright pink ribbed tank top that had white splotches on it.

Her hair was also now up in one of those buns that was damn near toppling over the side of her head—when she changed from her ponytail, I had no idea.

This wasn't a girl who cared what she looked like.

Not in the same way Jenna did.

"It was a knee-jerk reaction," I excused myself. "I'm sorry."

I could feel her eyes on me, and I glanced over just to check. Yep, she was staring at me and she didn't bother averting her eyes when caught.

Girl hardly even blushed, just pinched those cupid's bowed lips tighter.

I looked back to the road, fighting myself from glancing back at her again.

Which I ended up doing anyway.

Twice.

And then I shifted in my seat because fuck if her scrutiny wasn't making me a little excited...

Fucking pedophile. Who the hell got hard over a girl who looked like she was freaking sixteen?

She's twenty-two, jackass.

Still too young. Too young, too young, too young.

My head and mouth weren't on the same page, apparently, because suddenly I was asking, "Want to stop for food?"

And I didn't do shit to take it back.

CHAPTER FOUR

CALLIE

I HAD A FIVE-YEAR RULE.

I couldn't be attracted to anyone five years older than me. That was just weird to me. Girls who were into older men had daddy issues, at least in the circles I grew up in. I also refused to look at guys more than a year younger than me because I was well-aware of their immaturity.

So why was I curious about Trevor?

He was rude.

Who just blurted out in a room full of people, that he thought someone looked like a child? And then tried to steal that "child's" cookie...!?

A jackass, that's who.

But then he offered to rescue me from the house...

Well, I don't need no white knight.

Yet, here I was, sitting in his truck, allowing him to drive me home.

And then I agreed to food.

What the hell was I thinking?

After I agreed, it was silent in the cab of his truck. Not even the radio was on, and that made me uncomfortable. I needed to hear something other than the rumble of road, but I wasn't sure what to talk about.

I kind of felt like we had a "thing" going—he was rude but trying to make up for it, and I was the bitchy girl trying to ignore him.

But he was really hard to ignore...

All big, wide muscles.

Strong forearms.

Large hands...

I could imagine those hands as he murmured in my ear, in that rough, rumbled timbre of his...

I let out a huff. I had no business thinking about those hands on my body.

I shifted in my seat, uncomfortable now for *other* reasons.

"There's an exit up here," he broke into the silence and I had to stop myself from biting my lip at his voice. God, I didn't think a voice ever affected me the way his did.

I sat up in my seat and watched for the exit food sign, assuming I'd see a Smashburger or something along those lines.

Fast food but...better fast food. Made sense with a hockey player— 'nice' fast food.

A sign was coming, and the restaurants on it were fast-*ish* food, sure, but they certainly didn't have dollar menus.

Surely, he didn't mean to...

I kept my mouth shut though. I was thinking far too much into all of this. We were stopping for food and then we'd be back on our way. He'd drop me off at my apartment and be on his merry way, and I'd never see him again.

Oh, I'd dream about him, I had no doubt.

Shoot, I'd probably have a vivid sex dream with him in the starring role...

Not that I'd *ever* admit that out loud.

He was too old for me. It had to be some sort of fetish.

But oh my... They would be some damn good dreams.

The exit was coming up and the click of his blinker echoed through the cab. "Steak or pasta?"

So, not McDonalds, I thought, seeing the unmistakable golden arches off to the left.

"Fast is good," I said, nodding my head, hoping he'd take the hint. Micky D's wasn't on the road sign, so maybe he didn't know it was off this exit, too. "I mean, if you have a 'don't eat in the truck' rule, we can sit inside, but this doesn't have to be a thirty-minute thing."

"Steak or pasta?" he repeated.

"McDonald's."

"Steak or pasta."

"Dude. Dollar menu. All the way."

I watched as he grinned. "Steak. Or pasta."

"You know what? I'm not hungry." I looked out my window, crossing my arms.

"You're really fucking difficult, you know that?" He didn't sound upset by his proclamation though. The effer was laughing. "I want food. Real food. And you're not exactly dressed for some place fancy."

I gasped, swinging my head back toward him. "Well, neither are you!" How dare he? He was wearing jeans and a shirt! Not exactly fancy attire, himself.

And...

He was still laughing.

Effer.

"Steak or pasta, Cal?"

I slipped lower in my seat, before grumbling. "Steak."

If he wanted to be rude about my clothing choice, well

then, he could take me to Texas Freaking Roadhouse, and I'd have the most expensive steak on that menu! Take *that*, Trevor Winski.

But the rolls...

And cinnamon butter...

I was going to make a feast out of this. Rolls for days. Huge ass salad. Most expensive steak. Oh, yes.

Mind made, I sat up straight again.

Trevor Winski had no idea who he was messing with.

No.

Idea.

CHAPTER FIVE

Trevor

CALLIE MACTAVISH WAS a force to be reckoned with.

Just hours ago, I wouldn't look at the girl twice. Because that first look suggested she was nothing more than a girl.

But damn, I found myself intrigued with her.

She was a stubborn thing, too, and man, if that didn't have me curious to spend more time with her.

I bit back my smile as I maneuvered my truck into the large parking lot of Texas Roadhouse, finding an open spot toward the back of the lot. No sense trying to squeeze the beast into a smaller spot closer to the door.

Gives you a little more time to walk with Callie.

Yeah. There was that too.

I pulled the key from the ignition and looked over the bench seat toward her. "You ready?"

Her head was down as she was unbuckling her belt. "Mmhmm."

My lips quirked again and I shook my head, even if it was only for myself. I hopped down out of the truck and quickly walked to the other side, trying to get her door before she popped it open but to no avail. The girl was fast.

With her hand on the oh-shit handle, she lowered herself from my lifted truck with ease. Far more ease than a girl of her stature ought to.

When she made it to the ground, her arm still stretched above her, her shirt rose.

And I'm no fucking saint.

My eyes dropped to the generous sliver of skin and toward the center, a dangling gem suggested she had her belly button pierced.

I reached for the door, forcing my eyes back up and focusing on her face where, unfortunately, she wasn't looking at me but down at the ground.

It was almost as if she wasn't confident. That's what her body language was trying to scream, but her quirks on the drive said just the opposite.

Finally, her eyes lifted to mine and with her brows raised, she informed me, "You do know I'm getting the most expensive steak, right? I was going to keep that to myself, but I thought maybe you'd like an out before we sat down." She readjusted her shirt as she kept her eyes locked on mine.

Yeah.

Definitely not unconfident.

Maybe just irritated.

I could handle irritated.

"So long as you eat it, I don't give a damn what you order," I said, letting my smile break free.

Her eyes brightened and I knew I said the wrong thing.

"Ah. So, maybe I should order a shit-ton of food, and then just let it get cold. Huh." Her smile was crooked and, damn, cocky even. "Thanks for the idea, Trev." She reached up to tap her hand on my chest and shit, I wanted to hold her hand there.

You don't know her.

Nope.

But I wanted to.

So much for those earlier thoughts, because now that I had her here, I wasn't planning on letting her go. I was going to know who Callie MacTavish was, come hell or high water.

ONCE SEATED INSIDE, Callie immediately reached for the menu, opening it flat in front of her as she leaned into the table top. I reached for a menu too, doing the same, but glanced up in time to watch her bite the corner of her lip, and as it slowly, so fucking slowly, released.

Shit.

I knew in that *very* moment that I was going to ask her on a date. Didn't matter how much of a disaster this... lunch...might end up being.

I was going to ask her out. Twenty-two to my thirty-two, be damned. In the short moments that I'd known her, I was gripped by her.

By her blue eyes.

Her quick attitude.

I couldn't say the same of any of my other more recent relationships. I hadn't been "gripped" by them as I currently was by Callie. Of my most recent dating history, I'd dated a puck bunny—disaster in the making, but I didn't give a damn during the moments when we...connected—and a woman who was a year or two older than me, financially successful...

Met her during a jog.

Both those women had been fun.

Good in bed.

...But they wanted something different from me than I had to give.

They liked the rough guy on ice, the dominance in bed...but they weren't entirely keen on the gentleman act, or so they *both* told me.

Both of them.

I was too sweet.

They feared that the heat would die.

That it was all for show.

And they weren't exactly impressed by one of my closest friendships. A friend who happened to be female.

I was raised by a hardworking man who doted on his wife. My parents were a fantastic example of a great relationship. There was nothing wrong with being a good guy, and the fact that both those wanted essentially a *show* just went to tell me they weren't in it for the long haul.

It was often joked that I was looking for the perfect woman, and that I was too hard on the ones who crossed paths with me. That it was *my fault* they walked away.

And shit, there I go, thinking too far into the future than what was currently warranted of my situation.

I was going to feed Callie, drop her off, and probably never see her again.

Shit, I'd known Jonny for nine years; I was only meeting his sister-in-law now?

I could very likely never see Callie again after today.

The thought didn't sit well.

My friend Marlo's words echoed in my mind: *You think in terms of relationships. And not everyone is made for them.*

I'd been confident in that moment she'd been thinking of her own failed marriage, but maybe she had a point. I did think in terms of relationships. Shit, I wanted what my parents had.

What my buddy Caleb had.

Was I really reaching for straws? What was it about Callie that had me considering more with her?

If I really was the guy who needed to be in a meaningful relationship, was all this just because I was in limbo and wanted that relationship, and Callie was simply there?

"You're thinking awfully hard," Callie's voice infiltrated my thoughts and I glanced up from my glazed over view of the menu in front of me.

She was watching me intently. How long had she been looking at me? I ran my hand through my hair, flipping the freestyle to the other side.

"Debating chicken or steak."

She didn't answer, just kept watching me. I got the distinct feeling that she didn't believe me.

But how?

We'd spent all forty-some minutes together.

I was really fucking fixated on the fact we didn't know one another.

I was like some freaking pussy and that didn't sit well.

"Seriously," I finally said, tapping the menu with my index and middle fingers. "Debating on steak or chicken."

Her smile was small and knowing. "Okay." She didn't believe me, and how the frick did that work out?

I was left unsettled by a girl barely legal.

I was going to have to get over that, because I had a feeling that I wasn't getting over *her* when I dropped her off.

Not by a long shot.

CHAPTER SIX

CALLIE

IT WAS funny to watch a man as big as Trevor squirm.

I didn't fully understand it, no, but it was funny, none the less.

After our waitress came over—and did everything just short of sitting on Trevor's lap and gushing about what a hockey fan she was, which made him flush red, and me laugh—we sat in silence yet again.

Awkward much?

My attention was turned out the window while Trevor's was turned in toward the heart of the restaurant, where the staff walked around in their jeans and black shirts, the country music blaring loudly.

I ran my tongue over the front of my upper teeth, my hands locked in front of me.

I couldn't remember the last time I'd been on a date. Not that this was a date.

No, far from it.

This was a nice guy taking a girl home, and stopping to feed her quickly before going back on his merry way.

This was *not* a date.

"So, what do you do?"

Startled, I turned my head away from the window. "Excuse me?"

"For work. What do you do?" ...And then he had to go and ruin that good-boy image he was starting to have, by adding, "I mean, I know you come from money but..."

However, I didn't have it in me to be upset by his assumption. Instead, I shrugged. "I work." I turned my attention back out the window, watching as a car pulled into the open spot nearby.

"Like, what do you do though?"

Sighing softly, I looked back at him. I studied his face, trying to get a gauge on him.

Here was this guy—this sexy, big guy—sitting across from me. A guy who blushed when girls gushed over him, but still emitted that sexy, I can do it rough, vibe. I didn't know much about the team—I didn't follow hockey—but I did follow social media, and his name wasn't one that the media outlets flashed all over.

"Why are we doing this?" I asked for the second time in barely two hours.

I expected one of his non-answers. One of those follow-up questions he seemed to have a lot of.

I didn't get it.

"I don't know," he answered, and I could see the truth in it. "I honestly don't know. But you intrigue me, Callie, and I want to get to know you."

"You didn't earlier."

"I was a jackass earlier."

"Something we agree on," I retorted, partially hoping to get that cocky half-smile of his.

Instead, his face almost *fell*. "I'm sorry."

Well, that wouldn't do. "I was joking. Kind of..." I let my voice trail off but kept my eyes locked on his. Even though the lighting was on the darker side, I could see that eyes that I thought were brown, were really a combination of browns and golds. My gaze traveling down, I made out a slight bump to the ridge of his nose, then my eyes locked on the thin, jagged scar on his chin.

I caught sight of his mouth parting just slightly, probably for a breath or something, but it made me very much aware of this man.

His lips were full. I could imagine them on my body... up the center of my stomach...over my breasts...on my neck.

I jerked my eyes back up.

He didn't seem to notice my discomfort, thank goodness.

"Trevor Winksi," he said, startling me yet again, as he pushed his hand out over the table. When I frowned, he said, "I'd like to start over."

My half-smile was automatic. "Honestly, not necessary but..." I grasped his hand in mine. "Callie MacTavish. It's nice—" My words were cut off when he lifted my hand to his mouth and those very lips I was just fantasizing about grazed over my knuckles.

All while his eyes stayed locked on mine.

"Drinks."

My eyes widened and I jumped in my seat, pulling my hand back, as our waitress put our glasses down on the table between us.

"Your appetizer should be here shortly," she told me directly, her tone slightly condescending.

I didn't care whether or not she approved of my rattlesnake bites and fried pickles, but I wasn't a big fan of being looked down upon. I spent most of my life trying to be someone that I wasn't, and I wasn't about to start changing my habits for someone else.

"Thank you," Trevor answered, not once looking toward her but still looking at me.

Our waitress wasn't even fully turned before he asked again, "So, tell me, Callie. What is it you do for a living?"

I tipped my head to the side, and answered him truthfully. "I'm a pediatric nurse."

Knowing that he knew my family—or, at least, he knew my sister—I was expecting the shock that crossed his face. I wanted to sass, say that I wasn't as self-centered as my sister, but I knew that Trevor didn't deserve the reflex reaction.

"I'm impressed. For what, a year or so?"

I shook my head. "No, actually. I graduated from my program three years ago. I graduated my high school classes early and fast-tracked through college courses. But I've been at my current hospital for a year."

"Where were you before that?"

"Haiti for four months. Africa, before that, on a ship-based mission."

Trevor's mouth parted in shock, and I shifted in my seat, uncomfortable once again. I didn't like talking about myself, especially when it felt like I was trying to prove a point.

I did what I did—cared for children—because it was what my heart told me to do. I didn't do it for recognition. I didn't do it for God, or the church, or because I felt I had to give back.

I did it because I was meant to.

Both of my missions were with church-based groups, but I didn't belong to a church. My college friend and peer, Aimee, invited me and I absolutely enjoyed every moment.

"You'll have to tell me stories," Trevor answered, and I could hear the truth and awe in his statement. "I'm sure you have them."

I let myself smile. "I do. It was fun. I enjoyed it."

He sat back against the booth, crossing his arms as his eyes squinted and he stared at me. I forced myself to sit still and not shift under his scrutiny.

"Tell me," he finally said, "and I don't mean this as anything negative, I'm just genuinely curious, but how the hell are you and Jenna sisters?"

My smile dimmed in size, but by no means was I frowning. I thought about all the trips and gifts we received as kids. I thought about our parents, and how they were frivolous with their money. And then I thought about the children in war- and nature-torn countries.

"We just got different things from our upbringing."

CHAPTER SEVEN

"IT'S THE SECOND BUILDING," Callie said from the passenger seat, leaning forward as she pointed in the direction of her place.

Once again, I was surprised by her. Not only was she living in an apartment complex, but it wasn't a luxury one.

We'd spent nearly two hours at Texas Roadhouse, just talking about nothing, then about my hockey career and her missions.

Goddamn, was I impressed by this girl.

Woman.

She may have been young, but she was unmistakably wise beyond her years.

And I wanted to know more.

"What's your schedule like this week?" I asked, hoping it didn't come across as hopeful as I was feeling. I pulled the truck into an open space near her building and left it idling as I turned in my seat to face her. I unbuckled my belt to make it easier.

"Um..."

"I'd really like to see you again," I added.

"Well, I guess..."

It was funny to me, how she'd go through these little moments like this one right here. One second, she was sassy and busting my balls, then the next, she was almost timid.

"I have a game tomorrow afternoon, and then we're on an away trip Tuesday through Friday."

"I work twelve-hour nights," she finally answered. "Tomorrow and Friday night, this week."

"Shit." The disappointment was more than evident; the word was laced with it, and I didn't even try to stop it from coming out. "We have a team barbeque on Saturday; it's at Caleb's. I'd like to bring you."

Callie's laugh was light and she shook her head. "Yeah, no."

Her response had me curious. "Why do you say it like that?"

She unbuckled her belt and I watched the top of her blonde head before she lifted it back up. "They don't like Jenna, and therefore, me, by association."

While I could understand her thought process...

"I honestly don't think that Caleb and Ace would have turned my attention toward you, if they didn't like you. If anything, they like you better than Jenna. Shit. Sorry. That was a shitty thing to say." You didn't talk crap about someone's family.

Especially when you were trying to see her again.

Then there was that sassy grin on her face again. "Yeah, and you didn't exactly fall for it."

I held my hands up. "Hey! I brought you home, didn't I?" I chuckled. "So, I was a little against it at first. I thought we got past that."

She ran the tip of her tongue over her bottom lip, and I

watched the slip of pink pull back into her mouth. "How about you call me Saturday," she said as I locked eyes with her again.

Shit, with the amount of eye contact I was perfecting today, she was probably uncomfortable but damn if I didn't like watching the way her blue eyes held mine back.

"If you call before three," she continued, "I'll probably be sleeping, but if you want to hang out after your party or whatever, maybe we can meet up then."

She didn't think I'd call.

I got the distinct feeling that she thought this was ending right here.

Right now.

Not happening.

"Where's your phone?"

She frowned.

"Your phone, Cal. It's an iPhone looking thing. Silver case. Probably the girliest thing about you, from what I could tell today."

Her brows lifted. "Excuse me?"

My smile was wide. "Please give me your phone."

"I can be girly."

"Your phone."

"I'll show you girly," she mumbled as she dug into the bag she called a purse, pulling out the device before handing it to me willingly.

I was an Android guy myself, but I figured out how to get into her text messages. The first one on top was an unread one from Jenna, which I told her as I opened a new message. I typed in my information before texting myself from her phone.

I handed it back to her when I was finished. "I'm going to call you Saturday."

"Okay." She didn't sound convinced.

She was going for the handle when I reached out, putting my hand on her leg. It was hardly a brush—my hand was barely even touching her—but it was enough to send waves of excitement through me.

This was quite the surreal experience, hanging out with Callie.

"Let me walk you to your door."

She laughed lightly. "You really don't have to. It's alright."

I could tell that this was another one of her arguments, just waiting to happen, so rather than give her a choice, I turned in my seat again. I pulled the key from the ignition and dropped down from the truck.

This time, she waited until I rounded the front and pulled the door open. I reached my hand up and she willingly put her hand in mine.

"Thank you," Callie answered softly as she lowered to the ground.

I pushed the door shut and hit the lock on the key fob, putting my hand at the small of her back. She was really freaking tiny next to me.

My mind flashed to Jonny and Jenna; Jenna was clearly taller than Callie, probably by five inches. Then, I thought about Caleb and Sydney. They had a height difference.

I looked down at the top of Callie's head and decided she was probably a good seven inches shorter than me.

And then my mind went dirty, and I shut that shit down quickly, because the last thing I needed was to be rocking an erection while walking her to her door.

"I'm just over here. Apartment eleven-oh-two." She dug in her purse as we walked, pulling out her keys. I dropped my hand from her back when we reached her door.

I wasn't sure how to leave.

Wasn't sure what words to say.

Callie didn't give me much time to decide.

She quickly unlocked her door, pushing it open. As she stepped over the threshold, she said, over her shoulder, "It was nice to meet you, Trevor," and then the door was closed firmly in my face.

At first, I was shocked.

And then I realized it for what it was.

Her last word.

I barked out a chuckle as I turned to get back toward my truck.

Hanging out with Callie was going to keep me on my toes.

That was for damned sure.

CHAPTER EIGHT

April 2

TREVOR

I WOKE up from my nap, groggy as fuck.

I wasn't a great day-napper, but I needed the quiet time before a game or else I played like shit.

Rolling over to my side, I reached across the wide expanse of my bed, for my phone, sitting on its charger plate. Part of me was hopeful that Callie texted me. I knew that she had to work tonight, but I was jonesing to hear from her.

Surely, she was the same way.

I opened my notifications.

No new text messages.

...But there was an NHL Center alert.

I generally didn't pay attention to them before a game—they had little to do with what was happening only in a few hours—but this one had Enforcers in the headline.

I cursed when I read the words.

Fucking Jordan Byrd.

I opened my text messages, by-passing the name I really wanted to text, to open an older thread with Marlo. I'd been friends with both Jordan and Marlo, but when he left her high and dry with their infant daughter, I took great pleasure in taunting him with everything he didn't have.

Things he didn't have by choice.

Rori, their daughter, was five now, and an absolute doll. On more than one occasion, I plopped my ass at Marlo's house to hang out with Rori, giving the excuse that it was so Marlo could work on her cookie orders.

The woman was a beast in the kitchen, and made homemade cookies like nobody's business.

I liked to think that I was a positive male role model for Rori. She had plenty of them, as the entire team took in Marlo after Jordan left—because not only did he divorce her, but he was traded shortly after—but I spent more time with them than any of the other guys.

I was curious how Callie would deal with that...

The other women I'd been with, didn't care for it.

I shut that train of thought down—I wasn't even with Callie. And even if I was, and she wasn't supportive of a friendship—a friendship that was literally just that—then she wasn't as great as I thought she was.

Did you hear? Are you okay? Rori good?

I waited a few seconds, but the signs of Marlo receiving my message didn't pop up. I had to take a shower, so I rolled out of bed, sauntering to the attached bathroom.

Reaching into the glass-enclosed space, I adjusted the knobs to the position I knew I liked them best in, before turning to the sink. I put my phone down and started to go through my pre-game motions.

Brush teeth.

Pull out shaving items.

Shit. Next week would start the no-shave post-season run.

How did Callie feel about scruff or, because let's be honest, it was going to happen, a full-on playoff beard?

I shook my head at my pathetic self, then tapped my phone for good measure.

Maybe she texted me...

Nope.

Nothing.

From Callie or Marlo.

Letting it be, I turned and stepped into the shower.

I couldn't let thoughts of Callie ruin my pre-game vibes, and Marlo could handle herself. If she needed a friend, she'd reach out.

I had a game to get ready for.

CHAPTER NINE

CALLIE

"GOAL!"

I looked up from my hunched position on the couch and fixed my eyes on the television screen just as the camera panned to a huddle of hockey players pounding the hell out of poor number thirty-two—the only part of his jersey I could make out. Guy was being slapped around like nobody's business but they were all laughing like goons.

I wasn't even sure why I had the game on. I didn't watch hockey. Never had before.

And it had absolutely nothing to do with a guy who made me smile.

When the announcer continued, my eyes widened at the name used. "Trevor Winski is not a goal scorer, Mike, but he is on his A-game tonight! A plus-minus rating of four, two assists, now one goal, *and* this goal was on the tail of a five-for-fighting penalty."

"What was in his Wheaties this morning?" the second announcer joked, laughing through the airwaves.

The camera panned to the other bench—some guys in white, green, and red; terrible colors for a hockey team—before going back to the Enforcer's bench, where the guys skated back in. Thirty-two's back was to the camera and sure enough, in big, blocked out white letters, was 'WINSKI.'

I watched as he plopped down on the bench next to another guy, both of them laughing as the other guy took off his glove, reaching for a green water bottle.

The announcers were talking about Trevor's season while the camera was focused on him, and I took the moment to really look at him.

He still looked like the Trevor I'd sat down to lunch with yesterday, except maybe there was a red spot going on under one of his eyes, likely from the fight the announcers had mentioned.

And then he pushed out his mouth guard and smiled at his teammate...

Oh my.

Those straight, pretty teeth of his were not there.

Did he lose them tonight? I didn't even see the fight! But surely there'd be blood, right? They had on dark green jerseys, so even if there was blood, I wouldn't be able to see it.

The screen faded out and into commercials, and I had to shake myself.

Why did I care?

Shaking my head, I looked back down at my task. I had the coffee table pulled up flush with the couch I sat on, crossed-legged, and at the top of the screen, were the words, "Application."

I glanced back up at the television; commercial.

Toward my phone.

Trevor's at a hockey game. He's not going to be texting you now.

Back to my laptop.

It was an application I'd been filling for a travel nurse company. It would give me an opportunity to see more of the country. It wasn't the same as the missions I'd been on, no, but it would give me the chance to work with many other nurses in many different states. A nurse in our resource pool mentioned she'd done it before coming to the hospital, and I'd wanted to know more.

My experience wasn't all that great, though, so I wasn't sure I'd even have a chance.

But it didn't hurt to try.

So, before I could change my mind, I finished filling out the form and hit 'submit.'

AFTER A THREE-HOUR NAP, I pulled myself from my cozy bed at nine. I had to get ready for work.

In the middle of my applications and watching the hockey game, I received a call telling me I was cancelled for my first four hours. I'd never say no to an extra nap before a night shift.

Immediately, I went through my pre-work routine.

Quick shower. Scrub pants and a hospital long-sleeved tee; long-sleeved because it didn't matter how warm it was outside, the hospital was always freezing at night. Wet hair up in a messy bun, tied back with a headband fashioned from a bandanna looking fabric. Mascara to look awake— any more makeup would be wasted effort. Socks in my bag. Double check for pens and badge. Feet in flipflops.

I hit the lights in my room and headed toward the front door as I shouldered my bag. I'd just buy food from the cafeteria tonight, I figured, as I looked back toward the dark kitchen. I had to go grocery shopping anyway; I didn't have anything quick to grab.

Keys in hand, I was nearly out the door before I remembered my phone was charging in my room. I raced back through my apartment to grab it, opening the screen as I headed back outside.

Mindlessly—out of habit—I pulled open my text messages as I locked the door. Nothing recently received, but there was still that bolded message from Jenna from yesterday.

I hadn't so much forgotten about it after Trevor pointed it out.

I was avoiding it.

I loved Jenna dearly, but she wouldn't understand my desire to not spend so much money on our parents, and she'd eventually guilt me into paying the large bill. So, rather than talk to her about it...

I simply chose to avoid.

I tried not to feel disappointment at Trevor's not bolded message line; the last message was the first—the one he sent to himself to get his number in my phone.

Instead, I ended up opening Jenna's message.

Jenna: Just a reminder I need $5k sweets! I didn't tell you all about it, but we did save 300. They'll LOVE IT! xxx J

I sighed heavily, shaking my head.

I just...

God, Jenna.

She likely already paid for it, but she wouldn't stop hounding me for that money. Why the hell did she choose the *most expensive* vacation for them? Well, I knew why.

Had to have the best of the best...that was the MacTavish way.

Dammit, Jenna.

I deleted the message. If I saw it again, I'd just go into panic attack mode and I didn't want to deal with it. Not now.

Hopefully, not ever. I felt like that made me a bitch to think, but five-thousand was literally pennies in Jenna's savings.

Glancing up on my walk, I saw I was at my car. I unlocked it and slid inside, tossing my bag to the passenger seat. My messages now all appeared to be 'read.'

But one name kept taunting me.

I pulled the door closed and hit the lock button as my thumb hovered back and forth over Trevor's name.

You or he will text Saturday.

Don't do it, Cal.

Don't be that *girl.*

Swallowing hard, I hit the screen-black button and tossed my phone next to my bag.

Maybe I'd text him later.

CHAPTER TEN

April 8

Trevor

I HADN'T HEARD from Callie all week.

Sure, I could have texted her, but I was busy with our east coast trip, and I didn't want to seem too desperate. I was hopeful that I fixed any negative wrong-doings with her.

So, when my alarm went off at half past seven after only crawling into bed five hours before, my groan was there, but quickly put off.

I was texting her before she went to bed.

Better yet—I'd call.

I reached for my phone and, after pushing call on her contact card, lay on my back with my arm thrown over my eyes as the call rang in my ear.

Maybe she wasn't off yet.

I had no idea when her shift ended.

Shit.

I should have just sent a text.

Yep.

Should have texted.

I dropped my arm from my face and was lifting the phone away from my ear when the call clicked open.

"Hey."

I looked at the screen and saw it was indeed an answered call. Putting the phone back to my ear, I said, "Morning. Sorry. You're probably hardly getting off work."

"No, no, it's good." Callie's answer was quiet and partially muffled.

"Sorry. I should have just sent a text."

"No, wait. One second." There was a sound as if she'd put the phone down, a locker slamming, scratching as maybe she picked the phone up again, then the beep of… something. Time clock?

"I'm here. Sorry about that."

And suddenly, I wasn't sure what to say.

It had only been a week.

Shit, I should have texted her earlier in the week.

"Trevor?"

"Yeah, I'm here. Sorry. Just waking up." And her voice wasn't doing much for my morning wood situation, tenting against my sheets. I stared up at the ceiling to keep my mind off of it.

"And you chose to call me first? I'm honored." I could hear the sass in her voice and it made my lips curl up in a grin. There was the Callie I was starting to know.

"I wanted to be sure I caught you before you went to sleep. Didn't want you to have an excuse to not see me tonight."

"I'm not going to the barbeque," she answered.

"You don't have to, that's not what I'm saying. But I'd like to take you out somewhere tonight afterward." I placed my free hand on my bare chest, trying to picture Callie walking through the hospital, talking to me on her phone.

"I don't know, Trevor..."

"Please? With a cherry on top?" I added for good measure, earning her small laugh.

"Alright. Fine. How late are we talking?"

"Maybe catch a late movie? Hang out for a little before?"

"Okay. But I don't want to pull you from your team thing. How about you send me some movie times and we can go from there?"

"Sure. Yeah. I can do that."

"Okay then. That's a plan. I'll see you tonight."

I grinned. "I'll see you tonight." I was really fucking excited. Even my hard cock twitched in anticipation, even though it wasn't getting *any* action tonight. "Good night, Cal."

She laughed again and I could picture her shaking her head at me. "Thank you. Have a good day, Trev."

Callie hung up first and I held the phone to my ear a second longer, a shit-eating grin on my face. I liked the girl.

Unlike lunch the other day, tonight was a date.

I tossed my phone to the free side of the bed and pushed back my covers. The cool air against my engorged cock had me groaning and I slammed back down to the bed. Callie's voice echoed in my head and without even thinking about it, I grabbed hold of myself. I closed my eyes and pressed my other hand to my stomach as I slowly began to pull and tug on my length.

Trev.

I replayed my name on her lips, her voice in my ear.

I wasn't an overly-hung guy, but I had girth, and right now, I was swollen to the max. I squeezed hard as I pulled again, imagining Callie kneeling in front of me. I could picture her licking her lips, her lips parting, her mouth closing over the meaty head of my cock.

I squeezed at the top, adding a twist, and groaned.

I needed more.

I started pulling on my cock harder, faster, now imagining Callie's tiny, tight body over mine. I imagined what she'd look like riding me. High, tight, chest; breasts bouncing and swinging, because those babies were real; her tight stomach pulled taut and her little belly button ring flashing; her hands going to her chest to twist and pull at her nipples; her neck exposed as her head dropped back, making her hair brush my thighs...

"Ughh." My ass bunched tight and my hips jerked up as I came on my stomach and hand resting there.

I lightened my grip and slowed my pull, but milked the rest of my orgasm as I opened my eyes.

No Callie.

Just a white ceiling.

Still, I grinned.

If the *thought* of her had me this fucking exciting, I couldn't wait for the real deal.

"TREVOR!"

Barely seconds after my name was battle-called, I had a pile of kids hanging off me as Rori clinging to my back, Caleb's boys, Brandon and Brody, pulling on my arms, and Mikey Leeds' boy, Anderson, pulling on my leg, trying to get me to go down to the sand.

"Uncle, uncle!" I laughingly called out as every limb was pulled on.

"Never!" was the battle cry from my right. Brandon Prescott.

"Never!" his mini-me of a brother repeated.

Anderson tugged on my knee in the wrong direction, so rather than allowing the four-year-old to do it any harder, I exaggerated my fall to the ground, being sure no child was harmed in the process.

"We got him!" Rori yelled from behind, her sweet little voice a little too loud for my ear drums.

Soon, I was squeezing my eyes shut from the sand fight going on around me, and I held up a hand. "Alright, guys. We can't throw the sand."

I loved these "family" get-togethers, the ones where the entire team got together and the kids played, the adults chatted, everyone had a good time. There was a slight strain to today's, though, as Jordan Byrd was among us.

I wiped at my eyes with the back of my hand to look over the sandy area that was the Prescott backyard, toward the cement block where chairs and tables were set up. Byrd sat talking to Leeds; as far as I knew, he hadn't made an effort to talk to Rori, and that shit grated at me.

According to Marlo, he basically cornered her and Rori in public, when they were out with Sydney and the kids the other morning. I tried to give her an out for today; Marlo was more family than Byrd's ass was. She wanted Rori to be here though. This was as much her family as it was any of the other kids'.

I was fully expecting Marlo to call in her card though—the one that allowed her to leave, and for me to pull uncle duties and be sure Rori made it home safely at the end of the day.

So far, though, I hadn't seen her.

"Trevor! Catch me!" Brody yelled and before I could turn to sit on my ass, I had a running mass of four-year-old tackling me to the ground. I was going to have sand *everywhere.*

Laughing, I wrapped my arm around his tiny body and moved to sit up, giving the kid a decent noogie in the process. Sydney was going to find sand in the kid's ears, but that wasn't my problem.

"Alright, guys, I gotta get the sand out of my pants." I dislodged myself from Brody before standing, shaking the bottom hem of my shorts as sand fell to the ground, covering my toes.

I knew better than to think me standing and telling the kids to stay off, would mean they'd stay off. Soon, I had a monkey on my back—once again, Rori.

She was giggling in my ear as I laughed too; it was hard not to. This little girl's laugh was infectious.

"Look! It's Momma!" she shouted in my ear and sure enough, toeing off her shoes and walking into the sand, was Marlo.

"Let's go see what's up, butterfly." With Rori on my back, we walked toward the edge of sand.

Marlo smiled at me, although it wasn't a good smile. "I think I'm going to head home. Are you sure you're okay bringing Rori back? I can bring her home with me. Honest."

"Momma! No!"

I shook my head. "It's good, Lo. Honestly. Go home. I've got her."

"I just..." She shrugged and glanced back over her shoulder. I hated that that fucker had Marlo turning in on herself. It took her a long time to finally feel confident in life again, after her asshole of a husband left her high and dry after all they'd been through. "It's just weird."

"Don't let him take from you, what you worked so hard for," I told her, not for the first time. "You belong here, Lo. You know that."

She gave me another small smile. "I know. Thank you, Trevor." She hugged me quickly, then she reached out and tugged on Rori's now-crooked ponytail that managed to make its way over her shoulder. "Be good, bug, yeah?" I unhooked Rori's arms from my neck, swooping her to the ground.

"Yes, Momma." Rori hugged her mom tight before running off to rejoin the boys.

I watched Rori for a moment before turning my attention back to my friend. "Text me when you get home, Marlo. I mean it." I knew that nothing would happen to her, but she was emotional and I'd hate to find out something happened to her. Marlo was like the kid sister I never had; I worried about her.

"Okay. Alright." This time when she smiled, it was closer to the real deal. "Promise."

CHAPTER ELEVEN

CALLIE

WHEN I WOKE up at three, I eagerly grabbed my phone before I even realized I was doing it.

I was excited. Probably more excited than was warranted for a night-time movie. It wasn't like we'd be able to talk.

As expected, I had a text message from Trevor.

I pushed back to lean against my pillow and headboard, and quickly opened the message.

Trevor: Not a ton out but I'd be willing to do the chick flick ;) or we can redbox it.

Then, he listed a few movie times.

The thought of 'Redboxing it,' as he called it, was intriguing.

But he was a professional athlete.

And I was just a girl.

He'd expect moves if we were parked on my couch, and I wasn't sure I was ready for moves. I'd only met the guy last weekend.

Better to be safe than sorry, though. I texted him back one of the movie times, not expecting my message app to ping back as quickly as it did.

Trevor: Sounds good. See you about 730. :)

Thankfully, he didn't seem upset by this, if the smiley face was any indication.

Big, bad hockey player who was sporting missing teeth and the start of a black-eye when I'd seen his face on the television last weekend, and he was shooting off smiley faces.

The thought made me grin wide.

He was a special one, that Trevor Winski.

I slipped out of bed, twisting my sleep shorts back to their appropriate place. I had four hours to get ready.

I could tell myself I didn't need the four hours, but the girly heart that was fluttering in my chest was proving me to be a liar.

I was going to take all four hours.

No doubt about it.

CHAPTER TWELVE

THE LULL of the freeway was the only sound that filled the cab of my truck as I drove toward Callie's place. She'd texted me her address again, but up until I got near her apartment, I had the drive down pretty pat.

It was a fairly straight shot, after all.

During the drive, I replayed the twenty or so minutes I'd spent with Marlo just before hitting the road. Rori hadn't been feeling well when I dropped her off, and slept right through me bringing her into the house and to her room. After, in the kitchen, I got about twenty questions from Marlo about my date.

"Tell me! How'd you meet her? Is it the first date? Please. Let me live vicariously through you."

I chuckled at the memory.

Marlo didn't date much, and not because she was pining for her ex—I knew her well enough to know that wasn't the case. She just kept busy with a growing business and a five-year-old. The few dates she'd been on, she told me were good, but for whatever reason, the guys never called her back.

She thought it was because of Rori.

They were a bunch of jackasses, if that was the case.

When I'd told Marlo that Callie was Jenna's sister...

I grinned into the dark cab. Her reaction was a similar one to what I would have had. First, shock that Jenna had a sister. Then, bafflement that Callie was nothing like Jenna.

And yeah, sure, I didn't know her all that well, but it was obvious to see how different Callie was to Jenna. They were literally night and day, with the same set of strong physical genes.

When I left Marlo's, I'd planned on running by my place to shower but realized I ran out of time, which was easy to do when talking with Marlo. However, I now found myself regretting that I didn't make the time, as I drew within five minutes of her place. I'd been out in the sun and sand for hours and was probably a little rank.

Running my hand through my hair, I shook my head a bit, making sure there wasn't any sand lodged there. Then, with one hand on the wheel as I drove through the side streets, I pulled open the center console for the spray deodorant I kept there. After spraying a good dose on, I coughed and sputtered, dropping the can onto the seat beside me before rolling down my window.

Had to air the cab of the truck out now, dammit. *That was terrible planning on my part*, I thought, berating myself.

Trying to push the negative away, I finished the drive into her little apartment community, finding a spot not as close to her door as I would have liked.

Soon, I was knocking at apartment 1102, shifting in my spot like an anxious kid on Christmas. Last week, if Avery had told me this very moment would play out, I'd have laughed at her. Hell, I laughed at her when she told me Caleb wanted to set me up with Callie.

But here I was.

Excited as hell to take this girl on a date.

Not for the first time, it struck me how Callie wasn't like the women I'd dated before. She was different. Not just because she was younger than me, but she brought out a lightness in me that I hadn't experienced with the others.

All week, I looked forward to spending time with her. I cursed being away for so long, because I just wanted to hang out with her.

Then, finally, the day came and I freaking offered to take her to a movie. *Smooth move, Winski.* Nothing like a first date where you could hardly do more than hold hands.

Not that I wasn't looking forward to feeling her small hand in mine.

Maybe she'd even let me pop the armrest up, and pull her into my side.

Maybe she'd put her hand on my upper thigh, and I'd drop my arm over her shoulder, allowing my hand to play with her ear, her collarbone.

"Hey."

I startled. *Damn daydreams.* Callie brought them out at the very worst times.

Or the best ones.

I smiled down at her, standing in the doorway with her blonde hair down over her shoulders. A shot of lust flew through me. Last weekend, her hair was in a messy bun and while I could tell she had a lot of it, I didn't know how much. Now, I knew. It reached to just above her waist. I could wrap it around my fist...

"You okay?" Callie laughed, a little nervously.

"Sorry. I'm good. You look great," I answered, quickly roaming my eyes over her, which did nothing for the blood running south.

She looked down at herself before back at me. "I feel overdressed."

"God, no. You look great. Fantastic." She was wearing tight jeans with knee-high boots that had a heel on them, and a loose, flowing tank that looked like it was made of silk. In her ears were dangling earrings.

And here I was, in grey Hurley shorts and a black tee.

"I can change," she said, holding her thumb over her shoulder.

I had no doubt that she would, too.

I didn't want her to.

So, I overstepped a line that we probably weren't ready for, but damn my timeline when it came to a date I hoped would lead to more.

Yeah, yeah, I was often told I was a girl with that dating rule too—the no kissing until the second date, no sleeping together until the third date—but girls expected that kind of thing. It was all over their Allure and Cosmo. If you wanted a meaningful relationship, you took your time.

Sure, I wasn't exactly a young buck anymore, but I still wasn't all about rushing this.

But, damn…

I reached for the hand she held over her shoulder and pulled her near. She stumbled a bit at the pull, but quickly straightened as she landed tight against me. In those heels of hers, her chest pressed right near my sternum and as she tipped her head back, her lips were in prime location for taking.

"You look great, Callie," I reassured her, my voice low and, dammit, maybe cracking a bit too. "I'm the one who looks like hell, but things ran a little longer than I thought they would."

"If you're sure..."

"Positive."

"Okay." Her voice was barely over a whisper, and I had to fight to not kiss her in that moment. God, I wanted to feel her lips under mine.

Would she part them?

Would she brush her tongue over mine first, or would I be the first to make the move?

Would she moan breathlessly into my mouth?

"Um." Her voice shattered through my ill-timed daydreams, yet again.

I forced a smile down at her, all at once aware that there was no way in hell she didn't feel my erection against her belly, but if she wasn't going to mention it, then I wasn't going to either.

"Sorry. Let's head out? You have what you need?" Reluctantly, I stepped away, dropping her hand from mine.

"Just let me..." Her voice trailed off and she turned back into her apartment. I stayed on the threshold, waiting. Soon, she was back, a clutch-wallet in hand. "Okay." She smiled at me again, no longer looking like I scared the hell out of her. I took another step back as she pulled the door shut and locked it.

When she turned toward me, I didn't hesitate in taking her hand.

Hand-holding was absolutely acceptable first-date material.

Thankfully, she allowed me to slip her hand against mine. Just like I thought, it was small in my grasp, her tiny fingers threading against my thicker ones.

"I had to park a bit down. There wasn't anything closer."

"It's okay."

She walked next to me, confident and sexy as hell in those heeled boots.

I liked this.

I liked it a hell of a lot.

CHAPTER THIRTEEN

C ALLIE

DURING THE DRIVE to the theater, Trevor asked how my shifts at the hospital went this week, and I did the same, asking him about his games. I'd also asked about his black eye, which he told me never actually ended up being a true black eye, just a sore spot for a few days.

I didn't mention his teeth...which were all in place today.

He had to have fake teeth.

Which made me curious just how many teeth he didn't have, and if either Prescott had fake teeth. They were the only hockey players I knew and it made sense that teeth would be missing.

But I didn't ask.

That would be weird.

Hey, I saw you don't actually have all of your teeth.

I may have even had a semi-nightmare earlier in the week about making out with Trevor, only to discover he didn't have *any* teeth. It was...

A surreal dream.

Sexy. Hot.

And then just weird.

Therefore, I didn't ask because I didn't want to worry about what teeth he had and what ones he didn't. I was fine in my little bubble in which he had a mouthful or straight, pearly whites.

The theater we were going to recently renovated to all recliner-style seats and after Trevor bought both of us drinks, we moved to our ticketed spots near the middle of the theater.

I took my drink from his hands and put it in the outside cup holder, partially hoping—okay, a lot; I was hoping a lot—that he'd want to lift the middle arm rest up. When he put his drink in his outer cup holder too, I bit on my lip.

Maybe I didn't really want him to put it up.

Maybe...

He sat down and lifted it, before giving me a questioning look.

I could put it back down. I could tell him I wasn't comfortable with it.

No.

No, because I *was* comfortable with it.

I sat down in my seat then, drawing one of my legs up under the other.

"Do you know anything about this movie?" he asked in a semi-whisper. The trailers hadn't even started yet but I was thankful for the hushed words.

I shook my head. "Not a whole lot." I turned my head toward him. Even with the start of scruff on his cheeks and the scars and crooked bump in his nose, he was the most handsome man I'd had the pleasure of spending time with. "Just that it's supposed to be funny."

He nodded. "Good. I hadn't heard a whole lot either."

Then he grew quiet and I didn't know what to do with myself, so I took my large soda cup in both hands to take a sip from the straw. After I settled back into the seat and the lights dimmed with the start of the theatrical trailer section, I felt as Trevor shifted, then he slipped his arm over my shoulders.

"Okay?" he whispered.

I kept my eyes on the screen. I could feel myself blushing but I nodded. "Yeah. I'm good."

IT WAS A REALLY LONG MOVIE.

Funny during parts, yes, but really long.

Maybe that was because Trevor's heavy arm stayed over my shoulders the entire time, and I fought from leaning into his side. Oh, I leaned some, but not as much as my body wanted to.

I wanted to relax into his side, yet I fought against the natural pull to do just that.

I wasn't a girl to play games, but I found myself having warring reactions to Trevor. I liked him. I wanted to spend time with him. But there was a small part of me that was afraid.

I was afraid of the things Trevor made me feel.

I knew the man was attracted to me—he didn't exactly hide it. I could feel my face heating at the memory of his erection pressing against my stomach earlier tonight.

He welcomed my challenges, and met them with his own.

He made me smile.

Made me laugh.

And I'd only known the man a week.

And even though I never fully relaxed into him, not once during the movie did he move his arm.

He also never pulled me closer than I was willing.

After the credits rolled, we walked out of the theater, separate. He didn't reach for my hand this time. I knew, without a doubt, that my body language was too standoffish during the movie.

At his truck, he held the door open but kept his hands to himself as I climbed up—whereas when we left my apartment, he helped me.

Definitely gave him bad vibes.

I beat myself up over it as he closed the door and rounded the front of the truck. Trevor gave me no reason to be afraid of him. What was it about being with him that terrified me the most? His age? *So what?* It was a number. His profession? God, he played *hockey*. It wasn't like the sport would take him away from me. The fear that his profession would hold me back from my own dreams and aspirations, my own travels? That maybe I wouldn't be enough, because other girls likely threw themselves at him on the daily?

Fuck it.

I wasn't going to let misgivings drive me away from someone who had the ability to make me happy.

While Trevor climbed in, I busied myself with my seatbelt before forcing myself to look over at him, not actually bothering to secure the belt latch.

Mind made up, I swallowed hard before reaching for the center console, resting my hand on the front. "Does this go up?"

His eyes dropped to my hand then up at me, but then he looked out the front window as he pushed the key into the ignition. "Yeah."

Not giving myself a single second to think it to death, I

pushed my belt back over my shoulder and lifted the center console, scooting to the middle of the bench. There, I secured the lap belt without looking at Trevor.

I did see his thigh bunch under his shorts though, as if he was holding back from moving.

Then, after he'd pulled out of our parking spot and before I could talk myself out of it, I reached for his hand, placing our locked hands on my thigh.

He squeezed once.

And drove to my place in silence.

CHAPTER FOURTEEN

TREVOR

SO MANY MIXED SIGNALS TONIGHT.

Callie had held herself stiff next to me during the movie, but then grabbed my hand and put it on her thigh on the drive back.

So much for my fears of keeping date one within "rule book territory."

I'd be lucky to get a kiss from her.

Maybe this was why I didn't date younger women. For as mature as she seemed, apparently, she wasn't as much so as I'd thought.

Once we reached her apartment, I wasn't sure what to do. I'd walk her to her door, of course, but I probably wouldn't go for the kiss.

Not tonight.

Maybe next time. If there *was* a next time.

Shit. We were starting playoff season, which made my schedule a little bit tighter. Practices were more intense. There were a few more multi-night trips.

I knew I shouldn't have started anything with Callie.

I didn't have the time.

Not right now.

"I had a good time," Callie's whispered words filled the cab of the truck as I slipped my hand from hers and put the truck in park.

"Me too," I answered.

And I had. It was low-key and probably the most that I could hope for right now.

Callie wiped the palms of her hands on her denim-covered thighs.

"Let me wa—"

My words were effectively cut off as Callie took my face in her hands, pushing her lips to mine.

Not even wasting a moment to contemplate it, I twisted in my seat, pulling her toward me. She must have undone her seatbelt because she came to me easily. Then she moved one of her hands from my face to my lap...

My cock got excited.

But she didn't grab me.

Nope.

She unbuckled my seatbelt.

With my back to the door and a leg curled up on the seat, Callie straddled my hips like she was meant to be there. She cradled my face in both of her hands and rocked her hips against my growing thickness.

These shorts did shit to hide it, and I could feel damn near everything.

I groaned against her mouth and soon her tongue was playing over mine, the velvet smoothness dancing with mine. Swirling around, rubbing against.

I placed my hands onto her lower back, curling my fingers in to grab a handful of her ass, pushing her closer as my hips ground up.

The kiss was heated. Far more heated than I would have given a first kiss with Callie credit for.

It was hot.

Sexual.

Shit, I wanted my hands on her skin.

I slipped one hand up and under the smooth fabric of her shirt, my hand splaying wide over her back. Her mouth still on mine, she arched against my hand. I trailed my fingers further up her back until I made contact with her bra. I played my fingers over the closure, but I didn't make a move to undo it.

Later.

We'd have time to do that another time.

Callie's hands were under my shirt now, pushing it up my stomach as her hands swept over my abs, my ribs. Then, as her fingertips swept over my nipples, I wrapped my arm around her tight, trapping her hands to me.

"Come inside," she murmured against my lips.

Her breaths were heavy and hot against my mouth. We were breathing the same air.

I licked my lips, in turn, sweeping just slightly over her bottom lip too.

I shouldn't.

We should hold this off.

I didn't want just sex with Callie.

I was looking for more.

Sex tonight would cheapen it all.

"Okay," I said instead.

Still, Callie didn't move. She watched my face in the dimness of the truck before kissing my lower lip.

"Okay." She pushed away from me, scrambling to the other side of the cab.

Quickly, I turned off the ignition, pushing out of the truck. She met me in the front, reaching for my hand.

Then, as if we hadn't just made out hot and heavy in my truck, we walked toward her door. There wasn't a rush to our walk, but there was certainly a rush in my mind.

I wanted her sprawled out under me, her legs gripped around me, as I pounded into her. Her breathy moans in my ear, her nails scratching down my back.

With her free hand, Callie unlocked her door and stepped inside, pulling me with her. The door was hardly shut before her hands were on my shoulders, and mine were at her hips. As if this was something we'd done before, she hopped as I lifted, then I spun her so her back was to the door.

Our mouths were fighting against one another again. There was nothing sweet to this kiss.

Hot.

Dominant.

Wanton.

Needy.

Teeth clashing against teeth.

Callie squeezed her thighs around my hips, drawing me as close as I could get. I ground my erection against her center. God, I needed her. I needed to be in her. I needed...

"Bedroom."

Her hands were on my face, and she pulled back only enough to issue the words, "Only room down the hall."

I stepped back from the door with my hands under her ass, then blindly walked us in the dark apartment toward what I hoped was her room. Callie kept her mouth nearby, whether she was kissing my lips, my cheeks, my neck, nibbling my earlobe...

Finally, I found her room.

The walk was enough for me to realize that if this was happening, it wasn't happening like this.

I wasn't going to take her like some cheap date.

If I was breaking all my rules, I was still going to do right by her.

Shit, what if she only wants the down and dirty too?

I liked dirty sex.

I liked it a hell of a lot.

But I was struck with the need for this to be different with Callie.

I let go of her with one hand so I could feel for the light switch, making both of us wince when the light flooded her bedroom.

"Lights on," I told her, not wanting to get into that argument.

There was a time for lights-off sex.

This time wasn't it.

"Okay." I should have expected the challenging brow-raise from her, and fuck if that didn't make me want her more.

I took her lips with mine again, walking toward her bed. When my legs hit the mattress, I adjusted my hands under her ass as I moved to kneel on the bed, moving us toward the middle. Then, with a hand on the center of her back, I guided us down.

I was careful to not put my full two-fifteen mass on her. Callie's hands were still cradling my face, her legs still wrapped around mine. My cock was straining against my shorts, and I wanted nothing more than to free it and feel her, but I was content with this horizontal making out, where she slowly rolled her hips under me.

I knew without a fucking doubt that the moment clothes were gone?

This would be one of the best sexual encounters I'd ever had.

How, you ask?

Couldn't tell you. I just felt it deep in my bones.

I knew that this was a game-changer.

Meeting Callie, was a game-changer.

My mouth slowed over hers as the thought floated in my mind. Goddamn, I wanted this. But then Marlo's words came back to me. Maybe I was finding more in this moment than what was there.

I didn't have time for the girly-shit talk right now, so I shut it down and focused on *now*.

I rolled us so Callie was on top, but she kept herself pressed close, which was good with me. Putting my hands back under her shirt, this time I didn't stop to just play with her bra. I unsnapped that fucker. I wanted my hands full of her breasts.

Her mouth over mine didn't even falter; if anything, she ground herself down on top of me even harder. I was going to fucking come in my jeans if I didn't get her to stop soon.

I trailed my hands around her rib cage then slipped my fingers under her loosened bra cups, brushing over her peaked nipples. Her breath caught against my mouth and she moaned.

Fucking beautiful sound, that one.

I tweaked both of her nipples simultaneously as I kissed her back, hard. Her hips were moving against me faster now, jerking ever so slightly. She was fucking responsive; I was going to have fun with her.

I squeezed her nipples—hard—and her mouth gaped open over mine. I sat up and quickly pulled her shirt up over her head. She lost her bra just as quickly. Then I took what I wanted; her breast in my mouth.

"Trevor." My name was a breathless sound leaving her lips as she pressed her chest closer to my face. I braced my hands at her lower back as I nibbled and sucked on her nipple. Again, her breath hitched and her hips started to rock again. I moved to her other nipple, showing it equal attention.

"Shit, Trevor," she moaned. "I'm... Oh, shit, Trev. That feels so good. So good, baby. Yeah. Mmm." The last was said from behind closed lips. "Right there. Yeah." I swirled my tongue around her, getting her ready for the sharp pain-pleasure line I was going to have cross. The moment her hands went into my hair, gripping it hard between her fingers, I bit down on her.

Her body tensed, her fingers tightening, and I felt her hips and thighs shaking. "Oh, my God."

I soothed the ache then with slower swirls of my tongue before taking open-mouthed kisses along the undercurve of the swell of her breast. Once again, I moved her to her back; this time we were in her bed upside down, but fuck if I cared.

Her chest was heaving as she calmed from her orgasm, but I didn't want her to come too far down from her high. I crawled down her body, taking time to dip my tongue into the small divot of her belly button; no fancy dangling ring today. She just had a simple diamond curved bar. I flicked it with my tongue before asking, "You good?"

Her eyes were still closed but her smile was satisfied. "Yeah."

I kneeled between her legs as I lifted one of her legs, finding the zipper to her heeled boot. They were sexy as fuck, but they needed to go if I was get her out of her jeans. The *zip* noise echoed into the room and I glanced up at her. Eyes heavy and hooded, she watched, still looking quite satisfied and satiated.

Good.

I tossed the boot to the ground, then moved to take off the other. Callie lay in front of me in just jeans, her breasts heavy and her nipples wet and aroused from my loving, and it was a picture I didn't think would ever leave my mind.

She was fucking beautiful.

I needed to kiss her again.

I rocked forward, catching myself on my knuckles, and leaned down to take her lips possessively again. Apparently, she wasn't having anything to do with my being clothed, though, because her hands were at the hem of my shirt, pushing up. I broke away so she could pull it off and this time, I allowed myself to lay my chest on her.

The feel of her, skin to skin...

Shit.

As much as I wanted to watch her when I took her, I was going to be pressed all close to her this first time. I wanted to feel her everywhere, and I'd take feeling over seeing.

This time.

I sucked on her tongue once more before pulling away. Her moan had me chuckling.

"You better be taking off your shorts," she issued with a pout.

"Yours first." I winked at her as I resumed my kneel.

"Yes, please."

Again, I chuckled, then went to work on her jeans. These weren't just normal jeans, though. Oh no. They had six fucking buttons, and my damn fingers were too thick and clumsy to do it with practiced ease.

Three buttons.

It was all I got.

"Fuck this," I mumbled before grabbing the top hem, making sure to grab her panties too—I'd see her in them later; right now, I just wanted her fucking bare—and tugged.

Callie lifted her hips as she laughed. "Impatient, are we?"

"Fuck, yes."

Her jeans slid down her thighs easily but then got stuck on her feet.

"Fucking damn it."

Now, Callie was hysterically laughing, and I was too.

"These fucking jeans are like a torture device," I managed between my laughs. Callie leaned up and helped pull them off and finally, damn, *finally*, she was fully naked.

Her body was fucking beautiful.

And she had curls on her pussy.

I pushed her legs up and she draped them easily over my shoulders as I went to lower my mouth toward her. With one hand, I parted her folds and took my fill of her glistening pink pussy. Her previous orgasm left her wet, and I ached to lick her up.

So I did.

I took one long, slow lick, from opening to clit, before closing my mouth on that engorged bud. Once again, Callie's laughter was turned to moans. I could listen to her all fucking day.

Opening my mouth, I flicked my tongue over her quickly, alternating between flicks, swirls, and deep sucks. "Shit, Callie," I mumbled against her before sucking on the inner folds of her labia. Her legs tightened against my head when I did it, so naturally, I did it again.

"Trevor..."

"So fucking beautiful." I rearranged my body and watched as I inserted my middle finger into her waiting pussy. Palm up, I curled my finger and pushed it in and out. Watching her take my finger...

I could imagine her taking my thick cock.

Fuck, I was definitely coming in my pants if I didn't get this show on the road.

But I wanted to get another orgasm out of her. I wanted

to feel her clenching down on my finger, even though I knew I would imagine it was my cock.

I was thirty-two-fucking-years old, and I found a girl who had me having about as much control as I did when I was fifteen.

I pushed my ring finger into her waiting heat, too, and her pussy walls clenched down around the intrusion. Fuck, two fingers was child's play compared to my girl. She'd hug me so fucking tight...

I scissored my fingers in her as I pulled and pushed. When her hips started to rock again, I lowered my lips to her waiting clit, sucking and nibbling yet again.

"I need..." She was fucking vocal and shit, I loved it. "Yeah. Trevor, mmm. Yes. I need..."

Well, I needed too. Keeping my fingers lodged up in her, I moved up to kiss her hard again. I loved my mouth on hers. Shit, I loved my mouth on *her* but her mouth playing against mine was something I didn't want to give up. Not anytime soon.

The moment my lips landed on hers, I started moving my hand in and out of her quickly, allowing my palm to slap her clit.

She wasn't even kissing me now, but moaning into my mouth. I kissed along her lips, sucking on her upper lip, biting on her lower.

"Trevor. Oh. Oh. Trevor!"

And she was coming again.

Her walls clenched my fingers *hard*.

Shit. I knew then that the moment I entered her waiting heat, it was going to be a done game for me.

I slowed my fingers, allowing her muscles to push them out. She moaned at the loss.

"Open your eyes," I demanded of her. She did willingly.

With my thumb, I pulled down her lower lip. "Beautiful," I murmured before pressing my thumb into her mouth. Then, just before she could suck on it, I put my two wet fingers into my own mouth.

Between my mouth sucking off her juices, and her mouth sucking on my thumb...

It was easily the most erotic thing I'd experienced in the last year.

"Fucking gorgeous."

She smiled against my thumb and I pulled it back.

It was her turn to be demanding. "Undress. I want you in me."

"Yes, ma'am." I was off the bed and shucking my shorts and boxer-briefs in record time, my cock springing free and pointing toward Callie, as if I needed a reminder where I was going to be sticking it. I reached for my jeans from the floor, pulling out my wallet and removing the waiting condom. I'd like to say I put it in there tonight, hoping for this very moment, but really, it had been hanging out there for a few months.

Not only had my sex life gone through a dry spell, but add that to how fucking attracted I was to Callie, and this wasn't lasting long.

"Let me," she issued, still on her back and looking thoroughly used, as her eyes dropped to my cock.

She'd look even more used shortly.

I held the square package out to her, even though I knew I'd be gritting my teeth the entire time she was rolling it down over me, as I was pushing slowly into her, as she squeezed me appreciatively...

"Trevor."

Grinning crookedly, I resumed my position between her knees. Callie pushed up to sit, ripping open the package as she eyed my cock. It twitched then pulled straight up to hit my stomach.

"Excited much?" she mumbled, her eyes flitting up toward mine.

"Little bit."

Her laugh was light and quite the contrast from my groan as her small hand took hold of me.

"You're thick." Her fingers and thumb didn't even meet as she grasped the root of me. Slowly, she brought her squeeze to the head of my cock, twisting her hand over the sensitive skin.

"Callie," I warned, my molars ground together.

She grinned up at me as she rubbed her palm over the top. "Trevor?"

"I'm already not going to last long inside you. If want me to fuck you, put the condom on." The words came out far rougher than I intended, but I was a man on the ledge.

The words didn't deter her. "Hmm," she said, instead, as if contemplating. "Maybe..." She dropped her hand again, and started to move her fist up and down my shaft. My thighs bunched and my balls drew tight.

"Fuck, Callie," I groaned, dropping my head back. One minute. I'd let her play for one minute.

It was fucking torturous.

And glorious.

"I want my mouth on you," she whispered, causing me to open my eyes and drop my chin again.

"No."

"We have all night."

"No." I reached down to hold her hand still over my shaft, and the wench just squeezed harder. "Goddamn, Callie. I gotta be in you."

"Spoilsport."

"Next time," I promised. Fuck, the thought of her mouth on me would have me hard seconds after coming inside her.

She squeezed her hand again and I lifted my brow. I meant it. I wasn't coming on her hand, or in her mouth. Not this first time. Fuck that.

"Fine," she relented, and I removed my hand from hers. Then, after pinching the tip of the condom, she rolled it snug down me.

"Lay back." I was back to making the demands.

She did as I asked, a smile on her pretty face. I leaned over her, taking a moment to take her in. Her hair was fanned around her on the bed, having lost some of the waves she had in it earlier in the night. Her makeup was smeared. Parts of her hair were wet with sweat.

Fucking beautiful.

I reached between our bodies to push my cock down, feeling it connect with her waiting opening.

Then, with one sure thrust, I pushed all the way in.

Her body arched and her eyes closed. Her moan was a breathy little sigh of pleasure. She was as tight against my girth as I figured she'd be, and it felt so fucking right.

She brought her knees up to my sides but I as I leaned down into her, I said, "Wrap your legs around me. I want you all around me." She did, as I wrapped an arm under her back and other under her neck. She brought her arms up to hook around my arms too. We were a complete puzzle of arms and legs. I felt her everywhere.

Pressing my lips to her cheekbone, I started to rock my hips into her, my ass squeezing as I bottomed out. Eventually, her moans in my ear had me rocking harder, faster.

"Trevor."

"Callie."

"Oh, my God."

"Fuck."

"Oh! Right... There...!"

"Fuck, you're so tight. Shit. Feel you hug my cock, baby."

"I do. Oh, I do."

"Yeah, Cal."

"Trev."

"Squeeze me. Harder."

Her arms and legs and pussy did as I asked.

"Fuck, Cal. Right there. Yeah, baby. Like that."

"Oh..." Her breathing became erratic in my ear and I couldn't help but fuck her quickly.

"Trevor!" she called out, her body completely tightening around me, squeezing the life out of me.

And I fucking loved it.

Her pussy milked my cock hard, and two more thrusts, and I was done.

"Callie." I groaned her name as my cock jerked inside her, filling the condom in painful spurts.

So tight.

So hard.

So fucking perfect.

So fucking perfect.

CHAPTER FIFTEEN

CALLIE

I LAY ON MY BACK, my eyes glazing over as I stared at the ceiling light. I was alone and upside down in my bed, as we never made it to the pillows. Trevor excused himself to dispose of the condom, but being alone was welcome. I needed to sort through what just happened.

My breathing was slowing to normal, but hitched every time a flash of memory invaded my mind.

Trevor's lips on my neck.

His heavy breaths in my ear.

The sounds of pleasure he made when he came.

Next time, I want to see his face.

Next time.

I wanted a next time.

I swallowed hard and blinked away the fuzz. When the sound of Trevor's footsteps entered the bedroom, I turned my head, lifting my chin, to watch him over my shoulder. His body was made of hard lines and angles; he had muscles for days. Dark hair on his legs, short, sparse hair on his chest and stomach, a darker happy trail leading to...

He was hard again.

Or still.

I wasn't sure which.

I pushed up to sit, turning so my back was to the pillows and I could take the sheet and cover my chest, which earned me a raised brow.

"You okay?"

I nodded. "Mmm. Yes. I am." I gave him a small smile. "Were you... Um." I swallowed again. I had no idea how to ask him to stay, nor if he even wanted to stay. Maybe he wasn't that kind of guy. Maybe he was a wham-bam-thank-you-ma'am kind of guy. "Were you going to be leaving? Staying? What...?"

He stopped at the side of the bed, looming over me, a thoughtful look on his face. "What do you want?"

What did I want?

I wanted the pleasure he gave me, again and again.

I wanted to go back in time, and take Jenna up on one of her earlier offers to go to the Prescott house.

I wanted to spend more time with him.

I wanted...

"To use the bathroom," I blurted instead, to my absolute horror. Not waiting to see his response, I scrambled from my bed and out of the room. I didn't even bother grabbing my robe. I just hightailed it butt-naked out of the room where, if his low wolf-whistle was an indication, Trevor enjoyed the view.

I hated wolf-whistles.

I hated the men who used them.

But damn if Trevor's didn't make me feel good about myself.

In the bathroom, I did my post-sexual relations business,

then busied myself with washing my hands and face. Finally, bracing my hands on the sink, I stared at myself in the mirror.

My hair was an absolute mess; wild waves around my shoulders, amazing body in parts at my scalp. My lips were swollen—something I thought was only true in books. Timidly, I lifted one of my hands to brush my fingers gently over my lower lip.

My makeup was smeared and I was rocking some amazing raccoon eyes, thanks to tonight's pencil eyeliner, specifically. I knew I didn't care for that one.

I stood up fully and could see stubble burn along the sides of my breasts.

I looked thoroughly used.

Thoroughly loved.

Where the hell did that come from?

There was sex and there was fucking. There was no *love-making*. Certainly not on a first date!

A first date that I totally bombed by asking him to come inside.

Shit. Now the big bad hockey player would know I was available for sex and that was what this relationship would be about.

Who said anything about a relationship?

Maybe he didn't *want* a relationship. *And heck, Callie! You're hoping to be on the move shortly anyway!* I thought to myself.

I dropped my head back and took a deep breath through my nose.

I didn't know what I wanted. To stay. To go. To be with Trevor. To not.

Liar.

Truth—I was a liar.

I liked being with Trevor.

So why the hell was I pumping the brakes over and over again? So what if he only wanted sex from here on out, after I wantonly offered myself to him? It would be really great sex. It had been too long since I enjoyed a good romp in the bed, and I had a feeling Trevor gave it good every time.

...And then some.

There was a soft knock on the bathroom door, making me jump.

"You okay, Callie?" Trevor's voice came through the door.

"Um, yes." I looked at myself in the mirror again. Yeah. I was okay. I was good.

I was freaking great.

I smiled when I realized that wasn't an exaggeration.

But when I opened the door to find Trevor fully dressed, my smile faltered.

"I'm going to head out," he said, his hands in the pockets of his shorts as he looked down at me.

I should have felt uncomfortable—I was way under-dressed compared to him, after all—but it wasn't discomfort I felt.

"You can stay." God, I hoped that didn't come across as needy.

His smile was kind. I tried to read if it was condescending, too, but I didn't get that vibe from him. "It's alright. I had a good time tonight."

Of course, he did, the devil on my shoulder taunted. *He got to bag you.*

I fought against rolling my eyes at my own naysaying mind. With my heart pounding and probably too big for my chest—and therefore, contradicting what my mind was telling it—I shook my head. "I'd like you to stay. I mean, I get it if you have things to do..."

I had no idea what time it was. Eleven? Midnight?

Maybe he did other things at night.

Maybe he has another...

Thankfully, Trevor cut off that damned mimicking voice. "I don't want to do anything you're not ready for, and you're obviously uncomfortable." Then, he reached out and tucked hair behind my ear while looking down at me thoughtfully. "You, Callie... You're someone who's meant to be worshipped. Me fucking you tonight was a mistake."

My mouth dropped open but I couldn't get a word out, because he was still talking.

"That's on me, though. I should have known better. All night, it was obvious you weren't sure and the moment you opened that proverbial door, I took what was offered. I should have stopped to think. I'm sorry."

"No," I finally managed to get in. "No. Uh-huh. This isn't on you. God, no, Trevor." I was frowning but didn't care. "I wanted you. And I figured you wanted me too."

"God, yes."

"So don't put this on you. I did it." I hated that I sounded needy, but I had a terrible feeling that if he walked out that door, he may very well convince himself to stay away. "And I want you to stay."

His eyes crinkled at the corners as he stared down at me, studying me, those beautiful blue-gray orbs fixed on my face. It was in that moment that I was beginning to be uncomfortable being naked while he was completely dressed.

But I needed to play it cool.

"I'm going back to bed. I'm going to slip between my sheets, and I hope that you're not too far behind. But I'll understand if you have to leave. I won't ask questions; what you do when you're not with me is none of my business. Thank you for a good time tonight, Trevor."

I didn't wait for an answer.

I slid past him and walked back to my room, hitting the light and drawing the room in darkness before blindly making my way to bed. In the top drawer of my nightstand lived my sleep shorts and sleep tanks. I pulled a pair on over my naked self, and got back into bed.

I curled on my side, forcing myself to lay with my back to the door. I didn't want to watch it, hoping he'd come in.

The room smelled like sex.

Sex, and Trevor's skin.

I bit my lip and closed my eyes.

Please stay.

CHAPTER SIXTEEN

Trevor

I STOOD in the doorway of her bathroom far longer than necessary. I braced my hands on the frame and hung my head low, closing my eyes.

I couldn't do the mind games.

I didn't have the energy for them.

She was hot. She was cold. Then she was fucking on fire.

Only to run again.

I couldn't do it.

You want to do it. You know you do.

I lifted my head.

Damn right, I wanted it.

I pushed away from the doorframe, turning off the bathroom light before heading down the hall, and made my way back to Callie's bedroom.

The room was dark, but I could make out her body on the bed. She was facing away from the door.

You can still turn around.

Fuck that shit.

I pulled my shirt back off and undressed down to my boxer-briefs, then pulled back the sheet and comforter to slip in behind her. She didn't startle when I pulled her back into me. I could big-spoon like a pro.

She sighed quietly and looked over her shoulder. "Thank you for staying."

"You keep me on my toes, Callie MacTavish, but if you want something," I told her quietly, in the dark, "don't be afraid to shout it. I like bickering with you."

Her smile was small and I could tell, even in the dark, that there was more going on in that head of hers.

"Tell me what's wrong."

She stared up at me for a moment longer before pushing her shoulder to my chest. I scooted away and she rolled to her back. "You scare me," she whispered.

"Why?"

"You make me feel..." She paused, her eyes never leaving mine. "I feel more with you than I have before. And that scares me."

She stared at me a moment longer, neither of us breaking the silence, before she settled back to her side. Once again, I pulled her into the curve of my body before whispering into her ear, "You make me feel too."

I WAS HAVING the most erotic dream ever.

I could smell Callie on my skin as she grinned up at me, between my thighs. She pressed a kiss to my inner thigh before grabbing my cock, lifting it, then sucking on my balls, only to bring light kisses up my shaft.

"Trevor."

Her voice felt close, not hazy like in dreams. Then, her

tongue licked up my length and I twitched hard, my muscles bunching in my thighs. I couldn't help the groan that was rough in my throat.

The groan was real.

It had me waking up, opening my eyes.

The room was dark. It wasn't my bed.

"Trevor."

Callie.

Fuck.

Not a dream.

Shit.

Her hand tightened on my shaft. "You awake now?"

"Fuck, yes."

"Good. Just in time for me to do this..." I lifted my shoulders enough so I could see her between my legs, just seconds before she pulled my throbbing cock toward her open mouth. I pushed my legs apart, but my fucking boxer-briefs were limiting movement.

Callie didn't give me long to process that though.

She sucked the tip far more gently than I needed.

But enough that my actual need for *her* skyrocketed in point-two seconds.

"Callie."

"Mmm," she answered as she completely pulled the meaty head of my cock into her mouth, the vibrations having me bunching my ass cheeks. Her tongue swirled slowly around the head and her hand started to work me, up and down, slowly, as she sucked the head. Suck, release. Suck harder, release.

"Shit, Cal," I groaned. I dropped my head back to the pillow and fisted my hands in her sheets.

The *pop* of her mouth releasing me was amplified by the cold air hitting the wet tip.

"You good, Trevor?" she asked, no doubt repeating my very words from last night when I went down on her.

I tried to remember her response, tried to be as clever as she, but all I could manage was another, "Fuck, yes."

A small laugh left her lips and before I could open my eyes to watch, I felt as she took my entire cock into her mouth. She hummed again as she began to bob against my thick shaft.

"Fucking A, Callie." I released the sheets and put my hand on her head, fisting one hand in her hair and using the other to guide her gently. "Yeah, baby. Suck me. Yeah. Like that. Harder. Suck hard. Fuck, Callie."

I need to watch.

Shit. Yes. I needed it. I wanted to watch her blonde head bobbing, her mouth wide and taking me.

"I'm sitting," I warned her. "Gotta watch you."

She laughed against my cock and pulled away. Quickly, I sat up, my back to the headboard. Callie needed no prompting.

My cock was once again engulfed by her mouth, her head moving up and down, the slurping sounds made by my girth and her smaller mouth sucking hard, resonating loudly. I wrapped her hair around a fist again and this time, put my other hand on the side of her face, my thumb brushing over the hollowed part of her cheek.

"Yeah, baby. Like that," I murmured quietly. "Oh. Yeah. Uh." I closed my eyes briefly, trying to ground myself, to no avail. "Shit, Cal. I'm gonna come. Yeah, baby. Suck harder. Right there." Her nails dug into my thigh as her other hand squeezed tight. I liked her nails there though, so rather than tell her to, I brought a hand down to fondle my own balls. Her hand would be better but...

"Fuck, Callie. Fuck. Ugh." I groaned long and hard as

my cock hit the back of her throat, causing it to throb as my come jetted into the back of her throat.

Callie pulled back slowly, then sat up on her knees, a pleased look on her face. My cock fell to my upper thigh, still pulsing but sucked dry.

"Fuck," I managed again, pulling her face to mine. I kissed her hard and deep, as she sat there, smiling against my lips. I could taste my saltiness against her tongue.

I wanted more.

I slipped my hand behind her back and into the top of her sleep shorts, palming her ass. Callie moved to straddle my thighs and while it would be a minute before I could take her, I could definitely play.

But then the sound of a phone beeped.

I was ready to ignore it but the reminder beep sounded again.

"You or me?" I said against her mouth.

She shrugged, pulling back. "Yours? Mine doesn't make that noise."

Callie removed herself from my thighs and I groaned, which only made her laugh. "What time is it, anyway?"

"Five."

My brows lifted. "Why the hell do you get up so early?"

She smiled then winked at me. "I had a pretty heated dream."

My phone forgotten, I grinned and, after getting my briefs back up over my ass for mobility purposes, crawled over her. "Oh yeah? Who was the starring role?"

She settled against her pillows, smiling, and reached up to drape her arms around my neck. "Oh, Conor Mayweather."

I barked out a laugh. "Two different people, babe."

"Okay, okay, you."

I smiled wide then leaned in to peck her lips. "That's better."

Her arms tightened as she 'mmmed' against my lips. "Yeah."

I had a hand under her tank top, ready to move on to our next round, when my phone beeped again. "Fuck," I groaned. I dropped my forehead to her shoulder, squeezing my eyes shut. No one text or called in the middle of the night unless it was an emergency.

She raked her nails gently up my sides before tapping both palms over my obliques. "Check it." She turned her head then, to kiss the side of my head just above my ear. "Then we'll pick up here."

Not happily, I rolled away from her and off the bed, fishing my phone out of my shorts from the floor.

One missed text message.

Marlo.

I sat on the side of the bed, frowning as I opened it. It was time-stamped for three-forty-two.

"Shit," I mumbled after reading the quick text.

"What's wrong?" Callie's voice was near. She'd moved to sit on her knees beside me.

I looked over at her and couldn't help but imagine if we were in a more comfortable place, a bit further in this relationship we found ourselves in. I could see her hanging on my back, her chin on my shoulder, reading over said shoulder...

Someday.

No fucking doubt, someday.

"My friend's daughter was admitted to the hospital," I told her, knocking the wishful thinking back.

"Oh. I'm sorry. Is she okay?"

I shook my head. "She didn't say."

"She?"

I looked over at Callie then. Her face looked like she was warring on jealousy.

I dropped my phone to my side and reached for her, pulling her closer by way of her neck. I kissed her once, softly, before saying against her lips, "Old teammate's ex. She's like a sister, Marlo is."

"Oh." Callie's voice was quiet and I pulled back enough to look into her eyes. She still looked unsure.

"Marlo's ex is back in town and was at the barbeque yesterday. Marlo left and I brought Rori, her daughter, home before coming here. She had a stomachache." I pecked her lips once more. "I swear, she's just a friend."

"Okay." She smiled a little, but it was a for-show smile.

I didn't do reassurances. The women I was with either knew I was with them, or not. And with Callie's back and forth yesterday...

Shit, I was doing things all sorts of different with her.

"Callie. I'm with you. Only you." Then, I frowned. "If you want that, of course."

Her nod was small, her lips pressed tight.

"I did a bang-up job of showing you I want more than sex with you, but fuck if that's not the truth," I told her, lowering my voice. "I'm with you, Cal. And I don't share, so I don't expect you to either."

"Okay," she said again, this time sounding a little surer of herself. "Do you need to call her?"

"I'll just text. See how she and the kid are doing." I dropped my hand to her thigh. "Maybe you can meet them later."

Her eyes widened. "We... I just..."

The mood finally lightened, I chuckled. "You'll meet them someday."

She bit that lip of hers again then nodded. "Okay."

"Yeah," I grinned, leaning into kiss her. "Okay."

CHAPTER SEVENTEEN

CALLIE

TREVOR LEFT SHORTLY after our conversation. Right before he could text his friend, Sydney Prescott texted him to see if he wanted to go with her to the hospital.

I could tell he wasn't sure if he should leave or not, but I reassured him it was okay.

And it was.

Or, it would be.

It wasn't my place to be jealous of a woman he said was a friend.

I'm with you.

His words echoed in my head as I showered, the water cascading down my back. I had my eyes closed, just *feeling*. Feeling the water, feeling the heat.

It seemed to me, I found myself in a relationship.

I couldn't stop the giddy smile from spreading across my face. Finally, I opened my eyes, focusing on the plastic tub-shelling of my shower.

I really liked Trevor.

We hadn't talked about the next time we'd see each other, but he did say he'd call in an hour or so. He wanted me to go back to bed, but my body was humming with energy.

Trevor was, hands down, the best sex I'd ever had.

He probably had a lot of experience, given his age and profession, but...

I'm with you.

I closed my eyes again.

I'd never been with someone like Trevor. It was going to take some getting used to.

I wondered if the feelings he brought out in me would ever get old. Surely, they would. Eventually, right? Speaking of eventually...

I had to check my email to see if my application was received.

No sense putting the cart before the horse, but if I got this job, I was going to have to do something about Trevor.

Something like, not allow this to go further.

I bit my lip, opening my eyes.

...and I wasn't sure how I felt about that.

CHAPTER EIGHTEEN

April 9

Trevor

I PICKED up Sydney on my way to the hospital. Caleb waved from the garage as Brody pouted at his feet, Brielle cried from his hip—reaching for her leaving momma—with their youngest strapped in some funky-assed fabric wrap around his chest.

"You sure he's good with that?" I asked, glancing back toward my friend who had chaos going down around him.

Sydney laughed as she buckled her seat belt and I pulled out of their drive. "Mia is coming to get the oldest three in a little bit. He just has to feed them." Mia was married to Conor O'Gallagher, a guy I knew pretty well thanks to the bar he and his siblings ran. "Has Marlo called you at all this morning?"

I shook my head, easing my truck out of the expensive yet casual residential neighborhood and to the freeway that would get us to the hospital quickest. "Nope. Nothing since her text. You?"

"No." She placed her purse on the floor between her feet. "Just that Rori was admitted for stomach pain."

"Has to be something other than a stomachache. Your kids aren't sick, I'm not sick, you and Cael aren't sick. So, it can't be food poisoning."

"Who knows."

The drive was mostly done in silence then, until Sydney piped up, "I have a bet with Caleb."

Frowning at the odd announcement, I looked over but saw her looking out the window.

"Okay?"

"Mmhmm. Yeah."

"And? What's this bet?"

"That I'm the better matchmaker."

Again, I frowned. "Where's this going, Sydney?"

"You know I got my brother and friend Grace together, right?"

"Sure?" I answered, still confused on where this was going. It was too damn early for cryptic conversations with my buddy's wife.

"So..." I could feel her staring at me. "He wanted to try. And he deemed you his subject."

It clicked then. Everything Avery said. The side looks from Caleb.

"Yes, I'm seeing Callie." No sense letting Sydney draw this thing out.

"No!"

I laughed, glancing at her. "Yes."

"Shit," she mumbled. "It was because you drove her home the other weekend, wasn't it?"

"That was the start, sure." I tried to frown, but just the

mention of Callie had a stupid-assed grin on my face. "Do you not like her?"

Her brows raised, Sydney looked at me again. "Oh, no! I do. She's super sweet. It's hard to imagine that she's related to Jenna, but I do like her. I just didn't think she'd be your type."

"And what's my type, Sydney Prescott?"

"Dumb, busty, and middle-aged?"

I burst out laughing. Damn, if she wasn't mostly correct. "They were never middle-aged."

"Well…"

"Yes. I've seen Callie. We've been on a date."

"Will there be another? Because I can still win this thing…"

I shook my head, grinning from ear to ear. "Just give your husband his money." I frowned. "Or whatever the hell you bet; I don't really need to know that part."

"So you like her."

I nodded once. "I like her."

"You deserve a good one."

"Thanks, Sydney."

"…but if you could *not* tell Caleb yet, that'd be great. Maybe wait for next Friday."

I laughed again. "There was a timeframe on this bet?"

"Just…hold that information to yourself for a few days."

AFTER SURPRISING MARLO and Rori with our arrival—and assuring the staff that the Enforcers would be hitting the pediatric floors during our Back to School tour—I found myself sitting in the surgery waiting room with Marlo and Sydney.

Caleb came by with the baby so he could head to practice—a practice I was missing. I was sure there'd be some sort of repercussion for that. It was an optional skate before an away trip—Game 1 of the First Round in playoff season. So, definitely some sort of punishment, but if Coach wanted me there, he shouldn't have called today's practice optional.

I didn't have to stay.

But the second Jordan showed his face, going off on Marlo, there was no way in hell I was leaving.

Now we all sat, the quietness in the room interlaced with concern, worry, and a little bit of anger. Jordan sat across from me, a deep glare on his face.

The man had no fucking right to be pissed at *me* for being Marlo's shoulder. If he hadn't done the douche move and *asked* to be fucking traded, maybe he could have worked on his marriage, instead of taking the easy way out, leaving both his wife and daughter behind.

Every time I thought about the days leading up to his trade, I became more and more pissed at him. We'd been good friends, damn near as close as I was with Caleb. He did more than screw over Marlo; he screwed over the team too.

Now he was back, and I was trying really damn hard to not let my hatred toward the man affect us on ice.

Needing to change focus before I blew up on the guy, I looked over at Marlo, who was on her phone, then over to Sydney, who had her eyes closed as baby Brooks rested on her chest, his lips suckling at the air.

God, I want that.

The baby. The kids.

The kiss and quiet words I saw my friend and Sydney exchange as he dropped off the baby.

It was way too early to think that far with Callie, but...

I could picture her there.

In five years, in ten years, twenty, fifty.

Sixty, if I managed to live that long.

"I'll be right back," I told the room as I stood. No one answered, but Sydney did open her eyes a moment.

Leaving the waiting room, I walked the halls to what was called an outdoor Healing Garden. Once outside, I found a bench and sat, pulling up Callie's number, letting it ring in my ear.

"Hey, it's Callie..."

"Shit," I mumbled, hanging up. I wanted to talk to her, not leave her a message.

No sooner than I ended the call, my phone was ringing again.

Callie.

I opened the call, bringing my phone to my ear. "Screening my calls already?"

Her laugh calmed everything in me.

Damn, I'd needed to hear her.

"No, I forgot to grab my phone from my room when I went into the kitchen. Sorry. How's your friend's daughter?"

"Eh." I shrugged, even though she couldn't see. "Turns out she had like a hidden appendicitis or something like that. They screened her last night but didn't catch it. Then this morning, Rori was having more pain. Her appendix almost ruptured."

"Oh, no! Is she okay?"

"She's in surgery now."

"I'm sorry."

"Thank you, but she's good. She's a tough one. God, I needed to hear your voice."

I could imagine her smiling. "You barely left three hours ago."

"I know." I didn't want to think about what kind of sap

that made me. "We didn't get a chance to talk about the week. I'm going out of town again tomorrow."

"Well, lucky you, I'm only on one shift this week and it's tomorrow night..."

"Can I see you tonight?"

"Yes."

"And maybe you can come to my place Thursday. We get back into town early."

"Do you play Thursday?"

"Friday."

"Okay."

I let our conversation stall a moment, before saying, "I'd really like you to be there Friday."

"Trevor..."

"Please, Callie."

"Let me think about it."

"What's to think about, Cal? Are we doing this or not?" I ran my hand down my face. "Shit. Sorry. It's been a stressful few hours, and I don't mean to take it out on you."

"It's okay."

"No, it's really not." I chuckled dryly then looked up into the bright sky. "We can talk tonight."

"I have—" Callie stopped, then continued, saying instead, "Okay. Tonight. You can come over whenever."

I was curious about what she was going to say, but didn't want to press. "Alright. See you a little later."

CHAPTER NINETEEN

C<small>ALLIE</small>

I READ through the email again.

Then flipped to the other new email. Read it through as well.

Two of the three travel companies I applied for wanted to do Skype interviews over the course of the next few weeks. Both were impressed by my mission history.

I was equal parts excited and upset.

Excited, because this was what I wanted. It gave me a chance to travel again, and get paid to do it.

Upset, because I got the very distinct feeling that what I'd started with Trevor could actually *be* something.

Not wanting to hold off much longer on the emails, I quickly typed out a professional response, giving my availability for interviews, and hit send before I could chicken out.

Why was I so scared all of a sudden?

This was what I wanted.

I swallowed, then shut down the screen of my laptop just as a knock pounded at my door.

Trevor.

No sense worrying about interviews and whether or not I'd actually find a job placement assignment. One thing at a time...

And right now, that thing was Trevor.

I pushed up from the couch and walked to the door, unlocking the double deadbolts, letting him in. "Hey. How's Rori?" I made sure to remember her name. It was obvious that she and Marlo were important to him.

"She's good." He stepped inside and I closed the door behind him, only for him to pull me into a hug.

I laughed lightly, unable to help myself, and hugged him back. "What's this about?"

"Rough morning." He let go and toed off his shoes.

"Can I get you something to drink? Water? Soda?" He followed me as I walked back toward the couch.

"Just sit with me."

"Easy enough." I went to sit against the corner of the couch, but Trevor had other ideas. He reached for my hand before sitting down on my loveseat, pulling me into his lap. Then, he was nuzzling my neck from behind.

"So, rough morning?" I repeated, tipping my head to the side to give him more room to play.

"Yeah," he answered against my skin before pressing a light kiss there. Settling back, he wrapped his arms tightly around my stomach. I leaned into his chest comfortably and he rested his chin on my shoulder. "Jordan's an old teammate."

"You said." I kept my voice quiet.

"He and Marlo divorced and he left town. Five years ago. He's back, swears up and down that he wasn't in the wrong for not keeping in contact—"

"Wait. Didn't keep in contact?" I turned my head to try to see him better. When I couldn't, I attempted to shift in his lap but it wasn't until he loosened his hold that I was able to. "Surely he saw Rori."

Trevor's brows were raised and he shook his head. I could fully see how exhausted he was in that moment. "No. At least, not from what I know, or from what Marlo's said."

"Well, that's shitty."

Trevor's agreement came out in a grunt. "Anyway, he's back in town, with the team again. And even though the players, we're family, Marlo's also our family. Jordan left her with us, more or less. So Jordan's pissed because guys keep warning him off from Marlo, and because he swears Marlo kept Rori from him."

"But—"

Trevor's grin was quick, as was the kiss to my lips. "God, I love that you understand. But anyway. He shows up to the hospital all amped and shit, and I swear, he was ready to have a pissing match with me, and a full-on fight with Marlo."

"Why with you?"

"He has it in his head that I want her."

To that, I kept quiet.

He squeezed my hip. "Not going over that again..."

"I know."

"She's like a sister."

"You don't have to explain, Trevor."

"Apparently, I do."

I shifted again so I could straddle his lap, and shook my head again. "No. You don't. I'm sorry." I leaned in and pressed my lips to his, a little bit longer than his quick peck a moment ago. "Nothing bad happened, otherwise? Rori's good? Marlo's okay?"

He nodded. "Yeah. All's good. Right now, anyway." He

dropped his head to rest on the back of the couch. "What were you going to say on the phone earlier? You started something, but stopped."

I've been more-than-considering a travel nursing job.

"It was nothing."

Even though his head was back, his eyes were on mine and I could see that he didn't quite believe me. "Sure?"

I gave him a small smile and nodded. "Positive."

CHAPTER TWENTY

April 11

TREVOR

I WAS SO FUCKING PISSED at Byrd.

I had my own shit to deal with, this whole new relationship thing in the heat of playoff season. I didn't have time to worry about the hell Jordan was putting Marlo and Rori through, and whether or not he was answering calls from his daughter.

Right now, I should have been focused on the game, and about tomorrow's game, and then the fact that Callie was coming to my place on Thursday.

My mind was racing with things that dealt with Callie, with Marlo and Rori, with Byrd, and they weren't on the fucking game. It was Game 1 in the First Round. I had better get my head on fucking straight.

"Winski! For Byrd," Coach yelled, altering our line-up and getting our first line back on the ice. I stood and lifted my leg, resting my ass on the boards as I waited for Fuck

Face to skate in. He neared the bench and just as his skate was coming in, I had my own landing on ice.

I may have love tapped him with my stick in the process.

Fucker.

I skated hard to the opposite zone, getting into play nearly immediately. Leeds slapped the puck toward the goal; Texas recovered it, trying to shoot it out of the zone but the blade of my stick made contact, keeping it in.

I played with the puck a bit as I looked around the zone. Spotting O'Connell open, I yelled out and knocked it toward him. He answered the call beautifully, his stick raising and slapping down just in time for his blade to meet rubber, sending the puck in a different direction.

Unfortunately, it didn't meet net, but bounced toward the back boards.

There was chaos and mayhem going on behind the boards, and I stayed in position in case it became necessary to keep the puck on this side of the blue line.

Suddenly, a whistle was blown and O'Connell was ushered to the penalty box.

"High sticking," echoed throughout the arena as we skated back toward the bench.

I stood on the opposite side of the boards, still on ice, as Caleb and Jonny flanked my sides.

"Jonny, keep tight," Coach was saying. "Caleb, Jonesy, Winski, and Byrd. You're my four." I groaned to myself as Jordan stood from the bench, ready to get on the ice for the special shift.

"Winski and Byrd, no fists, no grit. Just protect Jonny." I knew who I *wanted* to use my fists on, and it sure as hell wasn't a Texas player. "Caleb and Jones, play tight and make magic. Don't get tired. Don't cause whistles."

Nothing like going into a penalty kill and knowing

Coach wanted you out for the entire two minutes but hey, it was why we got paid the big bucks.

Soon, the referees and linesmen were calling us back to the ice. We lined up around the face-off circle as Jonny crouched in net. Within moments, the puck was dropped and all hell broke loose.

This was the type of play I lived for.

The quick thinking.

The adrenaline rush of not letting the puck get through our shield.

We played hard for nearly the full two minutes, edging the puck closer and closer to neutral zone when suddenly, Jonesy called out and the puck went sailing by me. At some point, Caleb had gained possession and Jones was so open.

So fucking open.

The race was on.

It only took seconds for everyone to follow the path the puck was going to take. Jones wound up, shot the puck toward Texas's zone...

And a whistle was blown.

I looked around quickly, seeing red when I saw the likely culprit.

"What the fuck, Byrd?" He crossed the line before the fucking puck.

That was a rookie mistake. Fuck, that was a Juniors mistake! PeeWee mistake!

All that fucking work, for nothing.

We all headed toward the bench, but Coach waved us back out. I was getting fucking tired, but I wouldn't allow it to affect my play. Back to the face-off circle we went.

Unfortunately for us, Texas was the more rested team. They played with less mistakes than we did this game. It wasn't long before the red light was flashing behind Jonny.

I was fucking livid with Byrd.

We had it.

We'd been on a breakaway.

We could have had a breakaway goal.

But no.

He had to go and fuck up, just like he did with everything else.

At the bench, I kicked the door open and it crashed against the other side. The water bottles all shook in the wall but I didn't give a rat's flying ass.

No sooner than Byrd was at the bench behind me, I had him pushed into the Plexiglas to the side. "What the fuck is your problem? Huh, Byrd? Not only are you playing like shit, but you *are* a piece of shit!" Now that I started laying in on him, I couldn't stop. Years of pent up anger at him was unleashing, and his shitty playing was the reason I was letting it out.

"What the fuck are you talking about?" he spat back in my face, but before I could answer, Caleb had made his way down the bench and was pushing us apart.

"Break it up, you two. Not the fucking time or place."

Byrd's response was something about not knowing what my problem was, and I had no fucking problem calling him out, calling him a has-been.

"I said enough!" Caleb yelled.

I opened my mouth to say something else, but now Coach intercepted. "Byrd, ice. Winski, showers."

CHAPTER TWENTY-ONE

CALLIE

I WAS CHARTING at the desk when I quickly opened the web browser I'd pulled the game up on an hour earlier. The streaming Enforcers-Texas game was still going, but there were only a few seconds left to the game and the guys were down one goal.

I didn't have the sound on, so I couldn't hear what the announcers were talking about, but when the camera panned the bench, I didn't see Trevor.

Just a few seconds later, and the game was over. Because this was an Enforcers broadcast, the camera stayed pointed toward the bench as the guys all filed toward the tunnel.

No number thirty-two.

What did that mean? He'd been playing earlier.

It was only an hour into my shift; way too early to go on a break...but a potty break, I could do. Making sure my pager was on me, I headed to the locker room.

Quickly—my heart beating oddly fast—I opened up my

locker and grabbed my phone. I pulled open Trevor's last message, and typed out, **_Is everything okay? I didn't see you at the end of the game._**

He's not going to respond, Callie. If he's hurt, he won't see this for who knows how long. Shit! I hope he's not hurt.

I didn't know a ton about the sport, no, but from my clinicals, I knew all about sport injuries.

His answering text came in before I could drop my phone back in my locker.

Trevor: Just kicked off the ice. I'll explain later. Miss you.

I felt relief at the fact he was okay, but now I was curious about what happened that he'd been kicked off the ice.

My pager vibrated against my hip.

Shit.

I had work to do.

I'd talk to him later.

...but not before shooting off, **_Miss you too._**

CHAPTER TWENTY-TWO

TREVOR

I DIDN'T BOTHER SHOWERING YET, JUST stripped myself of my pads. I knew Coach was going to want to have words with me. Shit, Caleb was probably going to go on some captain speech the moment everyone filed into the room, too.

I wasn't expecting Byrd to be the first to enter the room.

He dropped his gear and stormed up to me, and even though I wasn't a small guy, with him in his skates and me not, he stood over me. I stood too, ready to hash this fucking thing out, when he put his forearm to my throat, pushing me back into the small divider between lockers. I ground my molars together, glaring at him.

"What the hell is your problem, Winski? You want my woman? My daughter? They're not fucking yours," he spat at me.

"Newsflash, dumbass," I said, my voice eerily calm but hard, as I stared at him. "They're not yours, either. I gave you the benefit of doubt, brother, but you fucking screwed up one too many times."

"You don't know what you're talking about."

"I don't? No?" I fought against pushing him back. "Who the hell did Marlo call a few hours ago, and *actually* talk to? Cause it sure as shit wasn't you."

"She didn't call me."

I was really fucking tired of hearing that excuse. "She did. But it was for Rori." I couldn't believe the man would turn his back on his daughter. Say he wanted to be there for her in one breath, and in the very next, ignore her. "You want to ignore Marlo, sure, fuck, whatever. You're divorced. You catch that part? Di-vor-ced." I let that sit for a moment before continuing. "That means she's not yours. But to be this close to your daughter? To pull the shit that you did at the hospital? And then not answer her fucking call?" I was done being held back. I lifted my hands to Byrd's chest and shoved him off me. "Fool's me. But no more."

I stomped away from the ass, shaking my head.

How the fuck could he turn his back on Rori, time and time again?

"She didn't call me!" Byrd yelled, managing to still get the last word, but I was done. I was so fucking done.

"Shut up!" Coach yelled out. The entire locker room went quiet. "Byrd and Winski. You two are sitting out tomorrow's game." I opened my mouth to protest but he kept going. "Figure your shit out." I didn't have shit to figure out. Byrd and I could play together, but we weren't friends any longer. That stopped the moment he made a douche move and decided his wife wasn't good for him anymore.

Marlo was an angel on earth and he'd been a fucking moron to turn his back on her.

I didn't stay in the room long enough to hear what else Coach had to say. I was done.

"SO. CALLIE." Caleb didn't even bother acting like he was reading the Sky Mall catalog in his lap. The damn thing was open but upside down.

"Yeah. Callie." I remembered Sydney's words and held back a chuckle. I'd play this out. "Ace told me you were trying to set me up. What was that about?" I pressed the button on my seat to push the recline back, looking over my shoulder. Leeds was out like a light. He wouldn't care if I was damn near in his lap.

"You drove her home. Did anything..."

"Dude. We're not fifteen-year-old girls."

"You need a good girl in your life."

"How the hell did I not know Jenna had a sister?"

"They don't get along all that well."

In the time I'd spent with Callie, we never actually talked about her family or how she was so different. "I can find my own girlfriends," I said instead.

"Look, I know she's younger than you go for—"

I choked back a laugh because yeah, that was the truth.

"But she'd be good for you."

"You're sounding like my sister again."

"Fucker, you don't have a sister."

"Well, you sound like a chick. Guys don't talk about finding good girls. They talk about banging girls." Which I would *never* divulge what happened between Callie and me. That shit was personal.

"I'm not telling you shit about banging Sydney."

"You apparently do it a lot," I said, grinning at my friend. "You sure like to knock her up."

Caleb grinned wide. "She's a good mom. And really fucking cute with a big belly that I put on her."

I shook my head, grinning. "Such a sap."

He chuckled and picked up the catalog, flipping it over and thumbing through pages. It was quiet for all of twenty-seconds. "But seriously. Callie. You didn't like... give her your number or anything after bringing her home?"

I grabbed my own copy of the catalog to busy my hands. "Nope," I lied.

"You lie."

I grinned wide, looking at him. "What's it to you?"

"Favors! That's what it is to me. Favors."

Now I laughed, I couldn't help it. "You and your wife are nuts."

Caleb gave me the stink-eye then, staring over at me. "What?"

"How'd you put Sydney and favors together? Maybe I was talking about something else. Like, maybe Jonny said he'd do something for me."

"Oh, my God, you're crazy." I put the catalog back. "Yes, Callie has my number. Yes, I've seen her. Yes, I'll be seeing her on Wednesday. And lastly, yes, your wife knows."

He seemed to completely by pass the part where his wife knew and we'd been keeping it from him. "Yes! I knew it! I knew you'd ask her out. Knew it. Fuck, yes." He fished his phone out of the seat-back pocket. "Daddy's going on a sexcation."

My body went cold, then hot really fast. "Way too much information, man."

"Shit, dude, Sydney's been holding out on going away

122

from the kids," he said as he started texting something quickly; to Sydney, I assumed. "Her parents *and* brothers have offered to take the kids for however long we want to get away for, but she has yet to cut the umbilical."

"I thought that was your job," I joked.

"Proverbial, asshole." He finished his text, then grinned wide. "Shit, to hell with losing Game 1 and fucking two. This totally made my night."

I grinned, shaking my head. "Yeah, well. Glad it made your night."

"I knew I could play Sydney's game. *Knew it.*"

"Sydney still has one up on you, though. Her brother and friend are *married.*"

He looked at me, a brow raised.

"Dude, it's been like...two...three weeks."

"I was in your shoes once. I knew after two hours with Sydney, she was it."

"Yeah, well, we're not all you and Sydney."

"I wonder if Chief will do another bet with me..."

"Like what?" I was grinning again.

Before he could answer though, a phone was dropped on my lap. I frowned before looking over my shoulder, where Jordan Byrd was standing. My good mood evaporated immediately.

"She didn't fucking call," he said, nodding down toward the phone.

I could tell the screen was lit up and he probably had his call log open but, "You probably deleted them." I didn't look at it as I picked it up from my lap and held it back out to him.

"She didn't call me," he tried again, sounding like a fucking pussy. "I'm tired of this shit, but she did not call me."

I shook my head, exasperated. "You're twenty-some-thing years old, Byrd," I told him. "Fucking call her yourself then." I was not going to be his sound board. I stood by Marlo's side for damn near five years while he played 'dip the stick' and got his kicks. I watched her heal from his leaving, I watched her become a stronger person, a stronger mother... I watched as she brushed off bad date after bad date, and still, she never gave up on her life.

Jordan being back could mean a shit-ton of things, and if he so much as broke a *fraction* of who she'd managed to become, I'd kill him myself.

"*She* ignores *my* calls," he finally said, thrusting his phone back at me. "I don't ignore her. She'd have to call me for me to ignore them."

This needed to end. I looked over at him, then down at the phone, only to shake my head. What a fucking asshole. I looked back at the blank screen on the seat in front of me. "That's 'cause that's not her fucking number, asshat."

"I think I know the number she's had since she was sixteen." He tried to fight back, as if he really was hurt about how this all went down. *He was the one who left.*

I looked back at him and his phone, then pointed to the screen. "That three should be an eight."

...and then I watched the blood run from his face.

"Shit," he mumbled.

"Yeah, dumbass." I shook my head again. "I have my own shit to worry about. Don't fucking hurt her again." Looking forward again, I silently dismissed him.

In my peripheral, I caught as Caleb looked over behind my seat, then back at me. "Gotta admit, the beef between you two was slightly expected, but it's a bit more exaggerated than I thought it would be. You guys are as bad as Brandon and Brody fighting over the latest remote control car."

I deadpanned him. "Do not compare me to your six and four-year-old."

His grin was wide and cocky. "Just calling it like I see it."

CHAPTER TWENTY-THREE

April 13

C ALLIE

"WELCOME TO MY HUMBLE ABODE," Trevor said as
he pushed open the door to his condo, which wasn't a condo
like the others I knew. This one was a single-family house.
Like Jenna and Jonny, he was near the La Jolla shoreline,
but unlike them, he didn't live in a place that screamed
money and glass and things that could break easily.

I stepped inside and was surprised at the homey feel.

He had rich wood floors with area rugs, leather couches,
and a huge television mounted to the wall. There were
some pictures out on a side table but otherwise the place
looked pretty homey.

"It's nice," I said, slipping out of my flip flops as he
walked in behind me, closing the door.

"Look around. I'm going to bring this to the master," he
answered, swinging my carry-on-style luggage gently. He

leaned down to peck my lips and I couldn't help but smile into the kiss.

Everything was so fast-tracked with this relationship. But then again, I felt like I'd known Trevor a hell of a lot longer than what was true.

My eyes tracked him as he walked away from the living room. He was wearing jeans that molded his back end, and a polo shirt that stretched tight over his shoulders. I could make out the bottom bulge of his triceps as he carried my bag—not that it was that heavy.

We'd done one video call while he was away, so I knew to expect facial hair, but when he showed up at my apartment a little earlier...

Some guys could rock a beard.

Trevor was one of them.

Shaking my head, I stepped through the living area and into what was obviously a dining room, with a gray chalk-painted, farmer-style table with four chairs and a bench.

He obviously did not do his decorating, I thought with a grin.

I ran my fingers over the back of a chair and turned to see the kitchen. Like the rest, it was open with an island near the middle. It had a second sink, even.

Brows raised, I walked back toward the living area and down the way Trevor had gone.

Nothing on the walls.

Two open doors on the left, one on the right.

The first door on the left was a bathroom. I peeked inside. Just a standard three-piece, but it had a door that went to the next room. I walked to the next door and saw the bedroom that the bathroom was attached to. Standard guest room. Double, maybe full-sized bed. A dresser. That bathroom door.

I turned to check out the other door, knowing that Trevor would be in there, but collided with him instead.

"Oh!" I lifted my hands to his chest and he covered them.

"The place is small, but it works for me," he said, as if he were self-conscious of the place. "I didn't need some fancy high-rise like some of the guys."

He *was* self-conscious.

I grinned up at him. "I like it. But you didn't decorate it."

"Who says?" He mirrored my grin, as he dropped his hands from mine to bracket my hips, pulling me so I was pressed even closer.

"Well, maybe you have an HGTV obsession."

"That, I actually do, so yeah, true, but you're right. My mom decorated."

I slipped my arms around his waist. "It's beautiful."

He nodded, looking over my head to the bedroom behind me. "She did good." Then, he looked back down at me. "How about a tour of the master?" he asked with a wink.

"You just want to have your way with me," I teased.

"Shit, yes."

I grinned, even though part of me was still slightly uncomfortable with the way our relationship started and progressed.

Trevor tugged on my ponytail, making me look up at him, before he leaned to whisper in my ear, "If I tell you something, will you trust me when I say it's not a line?"

I raised an eyebrow. "Well, that sounds promising."

He chuckled, then said as he lifted me effortlessly, "I've never brought a girl here before."

I wrapped my legs around his waist, my arms loose around his neck, and tipped my head to the side. "Really."

"Honest to God. I've only ever gone to their places."

I wanted to believe him...

Then I decided, that it was a decision I was going to have to make. A decision to trust him.

"Well then, I guess I'm special," I finally answered.

His responding smile made me feel good, as did his words. "Yeah, Callie," he said gruffly, "you're pretty damn special."

Conversation stopped then, as I lowered my mouth to his and he walked us into his bedroom. I didn't need a tour, I just needed him.

Unlike our other kisses, especially those kisses that led to our sexy times, this one remained slow.

Different.

He lowered us to the bed. "I'm going to take my time with you, this time. I want to know every inch of your body, every part that makes your breath hitch when I kiss it. Every move that has your pussy dripping..."

I smiled lazily. He was being all sweet and then he had to go and drop dirty words. We hadn't been together—in the relationship sense, or in the sex sense—that often, but I caught on that the man liked his dirty-speak.

I liked his dirty-speak...

It made me hot, to hear him talk that way to me as he had his way with my body.

I remembered the feel of his thick shaft in me, stretching me to completion. I bit down on my lip but it was only a matter of seconds before his thumb was there, pulling it down.

"What has you thinking dirty thoughts, baby?"

"I like when you talk dirty to me," I admitted easily.

His grin was lethal. "Oh, I can be sweet and slow, and still dirty. Watch me."

CHAPTER TWENTY-FOUR

Trevor

THAT DIDN'T GO QUITE *as I planned*, I thought, barely twenty minutes later as I lay sprawled on my bed with Callie curled to my side.

I had grand plans of going slow and worshiping her body, but the moment I slipped my cock in her warm, wet pussy, I was a goner.

"Apparently, we have to practice more," I finally said into the quiet room. Callie's answering laugh eased some of my nerves.

"It was good." She rubbed her hand over the right side of my stomach before pressing a kiss to my side.

"Yeah, it was, but it could be better."

Pushing up on me, Callie grinned wide. She was so fucking beautiful, completely carefree in the fact she was nude. There wasn't a rush to cover up with sheets. No. She sat there, perched on her hip with her hair down and wild, the slightest pooch to her stomach where she sat curled, her tits out and her nipples smooth...

So many women had issues with being naked. They all wanted perky breasts and popped nipples, smooth stomachs —like that was what made them sexy.

This.

Callie.

She was sexy.

She *owned* her sexy.

She ran her finger down the center of my chest and rather than watch her finger, I watched her eyes. *She* was watching her finger travel down, down, down...and I felt her grab my still chubby cock. There just was no such thing as soft when I was in bed with her; I was always just about ready to go.

Still, she didn't look at me.

"I want to feel you bare against me. In me," she finally said, her thumb rubbing up and down my shaft slowly. I could feel myself stiffening in her hand, mostly from the stimulation but fuck, the idea of feeling her all around me...

"Shit, I wouldn't last two seconds."

She grinned wide, a little crooked, and finally brought her eyes to mine. "That's what practice is for."

"I'm clean."

"I'm on the pill."

"Then fuck, yes." I was a greedy, horny boy. I'd absolutely take her bare.

"And this," she said, dropping my cock to my stomach and reaching up to my face. "I want to feel this between my thighs," she whispered as her fingers brushed over my growing-in beard.

I'd been so fucking excited to be with her, and she'd been so wet and ready, there was no foreplay. Her telling me she wanted my beard against her had me salivating to take her. To put my mouth against her.

With a growl, I flipped her to her back—and she

laughed the entire time. That is, until I rotated her body so I could kneel on the ground, my face eye level with her waiting, wanting pussy, and put my mouth on her.

"Trevor..." I loved her breathy way of saying my name. Fucking loved it.

I hummed against her, moving my mouth and tongue around her slick folds. I alternated between sucking on her clit and fucking her with my tongue. Her hips were writhing against my face, her hands were on my head, keeping me pressed right into the apex of her thighs.

"Yeah. That. Like that," she issued when I went back to her clit, letting my chin rub against her too.

"Oh, yes," she said again. "That. Right there. Mmhmm. Mmhmm." Her answering mmhmms were getting higher pitched with each one.

She was right there.

And I knew I wasn't going to last our first time without latex between us.

Quickly, I stood, taking her spread legs in my hands and thrust deep into her.

"Oh, my God!" Her body arched at the intrusion; there was no whispered sigh this time. No, this was an immediate push over her peak and into an orgasm.

"Fuck, Callie," I muttered, thrusting my hips quickly. Watching her was everything I thought it would be. Her face tightened when she was coming, and she had the smallest frown line between her brows, as if she were concentrating on keeping the wave rolling.

I could help with that.

I slid my hands down her inner thighs, still holding her legs apart, and splayed one out wide so my thumb could roll over her clit.

"Shit, Trevor." Her body shook again, her thighs quivering under my hands.

"Yeah, baby. Keep squeezing. That feels so good. Yeah, Cal," I muttered, my own face starting to pinch tight as I fought to keep myself from coming.

But she was so fucking wet.

Her pussy so freaking smooth against my cock.

And her orgasm had her squeezing me again and again, so fucking tight.

Her body arched one more time and I couldn't hold it any longer. "Shit, Callie. Fuck!" My body jerked hard, pushing my cock all the way in, our pelvises meeting in a hot, wet kiss. Her cum was soaking my groin and fuck, if that wasn't hot as shit.

I grunted again as my hands loosened on her thighs, then dropped down so I could pull her close, my mouth getting some action now. The kiss was heated, but slow as we both fought to catch our breaths.

I'd been with women before who I was good with one time and done.

Not even a handful of times with her, and I knew I wanted more. Would want more.

Sex with Callie would never get old.

I had no fucking doubt.

CHAPTER TWENTY-FIVE

C<small>ALLIE</small>

"HOW ARE you so different from Jenna?"

I opened my eyes at the question. I'd been half-asleep, my back to Trevor's front, as we lounged in his fancy soaker tub.

I shifted so I could look up at him over my shoulder. His chin was dropped so he could watch me, his eyes slightly heavy-lidded as if he, too, had been in a deep relaxed state before asking. He tightened his locked hands over my stomach, as if he were afraid that my moving would mean me leaving.

I'm not going anywhere, I thought.

"What do you mean?" I asked, even though the question was straight-forward.

"You're just nothing like her."

I settled back against his chest and his hands loosened again. "We just got different things out of our upraising," I finally answered. Trevor splayed a hand over my stomach and used the other to draw light circles up and down my side. "We went on vacations, and she saw parties and music and beaches, where I saw the homeless kids on the corner. We went to a function for a charity, and she saw people with heavy pockets, while I was researching the charity." I shrugged. "She is how we were raised."

"You're empathetic."

I closed my eyes and smiled lightly. "That's a big word for a hockey player."

I could feel his chuckle, but his words were not as light. "I'm being serious."

"I know." I sighed happily, content to be right here, like this, until the water ran cold. "She has good intentions," I finally said, thinking about the trip she had us sending our parents on. It was something our parents would enjoy, and that's what Jenna saw. She didn't notice price tags, although she did prefer the biggest ones. "And I think," I started, but quickly stopped because I wasn't sure how it would be taken.

"What?"

I wanted to keep my eyes closed to try and block everything out, but because I started it... "I think that she's stand-offish with the team and the Prescotts because while we all have money, the Prescotts treat theirs differently." They treated it how I did, to be honest. "And I also think that she's with Jonny for the wrong reasons."

That seemed to take Trevor aback. "Why?"

I puffed out my cheeks and opened my eyes, trying to figure out how to say it. I thought back to when we were younger, to when Jenna was sixteen. I was barely ten, so I didn't think much of it at the time, but it was something that sometimes knocked on the back of my mind. "Jonny and Jenna broke up sometime in high school. *She* broke up with him, actually. I remember she was getting ready to go to prom with a family friend, a guy whose first car was a Porsche." I laughed lightly, remembering Jenna's excitement over this new guy. "Sixteen and a Porsche. Anyway. It was the day before—or maybe the day of—prom, and she comes home from wherever she was, shouting in excitement that Jonny was selected for a Juniors team." I hadn't known much about hockey then, but I since came to understand that Juniors was the league for the really good young kids, before colleges and professional teams considered picking them up. It was the elite of the elite. "Everyone knew that the Prescott boys had a chance at the NHL, and that really just seemed to solidify Jonny's future. Prom came, and it wasn't the boy with the Porsche that Jenna went with."

"So, you think she's with him because he was basically destined to be well-off."

I cringed. It sounded so much worse being repeated to me. "That makes me a horrible sister, to admit to that."

Trevor was quiet and I chewed on my lip, afraid that what I had said would somehow reflect badly on me. "It makes sense," he finally said, just as I was getting antsy to move. "It makes a lot of sense, actually," he said again. I looked over my shoulder to see he had a thoughtful expression on his face as he stared at the slate-tiled wall across from us.

"I feel bad saying it," I admitted, my voice quiet. "Jonny's always been good to our family. I just hate the thought that maybe my sister hasn't always been good for Jonny."

Trevor brought his eyes to mine then, shrugging a big shoulder. "He's a big boy. We all do what we want in the end, anyway."

I nodded slightly. "Yeah."

"You want to know what I want to do?" he asked, a wicked gleam in his eye.

If his intention was to get me to smile, he managed to do it. I had an idea but still asked, "What's that?"

"You." He playfully bit my shoulder. "I get you to myself for the next eighteen hours, before life intervenes. I'm using every single minute."

CHAPTER TWENTY-SIX

April 14

TREVOR

THIS WENT against absolutely every pre-game ritual I had but, "Fuck, Callie," I groaned as she sat on top of me, my cock straight up and down as she rubbed herself over it.

My she-devil smiled down at me but I dropped my eyes back down to my hips. It was a sight, her fingers against my cock, holding the hard length against her pink folds as she rolled her hips up and down.

She moaned—and bit her lip; I had to look up to catch that sexy little move—when the head of my cock rubbed her clit. I kept slipping against her folds and the more she rolled, the more I just wanted to be *in* her.

I gripped her hips hard. "Callie," I warned.

"We're practicing," she murmured. "You have to get used to the stimulation."

I laughed, even though I was on edge. "You're so fucking sassy."

"I think maybe," she stated, rolling her hips again. My cock was wrapped by pussy lips and fingers, and shit, it was erotic. "Maybe we should do this for a few more minutes."

"Oh, fuck no," I answered, not sure if she was kidding or not. "Fuck. No." The last was on a groan. "Shit, Callie." Finally, I could take no more. I was *not* shooting my load against her stomach, not when I was going to have to get ready for my game in less than an hour.

Fuck.

No.

I was done being the bottom. She had her fun; now it was my turn.

With my hands on her hips, I wrapped my arms around her and flipped us, Callie laughing the entire time. I lined my cock up with her waiting pussy, and then gave her a taste of her own medicine.

I inched in her. One slow inch.

Then out.

A little bit more.

Then all. Of the way. The fuck. Out.

"Trevor," she whined.

"I think we should get you used to my size," I taunted her.

"Don't be mean." Her pout was fake, and she crunched up so she could reach my ass, her nails digging in. I pushed back against her, my cock notched in her but going nowhere, no matter how hard she tried to pull me closer.

"Trevor...!"

"Callie!" I couldn't help but laugh.

"Please, Trevor."

"You done teasing?"

"Yes. Please." Her nails dug in to my muscles.

"If you're sure..." I could keep this going.

Well, not for too much longer, I thought as the green

139

numbers on my alarm clock teased me from the bedside table.

"Please," she said again and that time, I pushed all the way in—slowly, still. I wanted to feel as her walls and muscles pulled at me.

Her moan was simultaneous with my groan. It was fucking perfect.

"Yeah, baby."

Her hands dropped from my ass, clutching the sheet below her, as her eyes closed.

"How do you want it?" I asked, rolling my hips against hers, my cock stirring against her tight pussy.

"Like that. Yeah, mmm."

"Open your eyes, Cal."

She did immediately. Her pupils were wide and it looked like she had to take a moment to focus. Overnight, I learned her body, her reactions, well. There was very little rest for us, and I'd probably be regretting it—only a little—as I played in a few hours, but I wouldn't trade this time for a second.

I kept rolling my hips into hers, my cock pulling through her slick heat slowly.

"Play with your tits," I demanded. "Twist your nipples for me. I want to watch."

She brought her hands to her chest and rolled her nipples between her thumbs and index fingers, an answering sigh shortly after.

"Yeah, baby. Like that. Roll them a little harder. Pinch one. Pinch it hard now," I issued, pushing my thick girth fully into her.

Her answers were always my name, and I fucking loved it. Her legs began to tremble but I could see her fighting to hold off her orgasm.

I could work with that...

But I was going to change things up in the meantime.

Pausing my movements, I took her legs and braced her feet on my chest before giving her a small thrust. "What about that, Callie? How's that feel?"

"Tighter," she moaned. "So good."

"Yeah, Callie. So good," I echoed, starting to move again. I squeezed her ankles as I rocked against her. "Take my thick cock like that. Yeah. Like that."

She stopped squeezing her nipples, but she did keep herself going by rubbing her thumb in slow circles over one peak. Her eyes were getting heavy again; she wanted to close her eyes and just feel.

I could do that for her.

"Close those pretty eyes, baby."

She did, without question.

"Feel it. Feel all of it." Then I lifted one of her feet from my chest to suck on her toe.

"Ohmigod," she moaned quietly. "Trev..."

"Keep your eyes closed." My hips kept with their slow dance and I ran my nose up the arch of her foot. "How's that for getting used to stimulation," I teased.

"Trevor." She opened her eyes.

"Uh-uh."

She closed them again and I rewarded her by sucking on her toe again. I had a feeling that the nerve endings, paired with hands on her chest, and my cock in her pussy...

"Yeah..." she moaned.

"Oh, yes."

Her breathing quickened and I sucked one more time, just as I pushed in.

"Trevor!" she called out, her orgasm taking over.

"That's it, baby," I praised. Carefully, I rearranged her legs back down so I could lean over her, resting my body on hers. "Milk my cock with your cum. Yeah, baby." My thrusts were getting quicker; I wasn't going to hold off much longer.

I needed...

I buried my head against her neck and allowed my basic animal needs to take over, pounding my hips into her hard and fast, my balls slapping her ass and adding to the sloppy love making noises. Her breaths and moans egged me on, telling me to take her harder, *harder*, faster, deeper...

"Fuck!" I groaned, as there was nearly zero warning between the tingle in my spine, the tightening of my balls, and my cum shooting into her waiting heat. "Shit," I bit on another grunt.

"God..." I took a deep breath into the pillow under Callie's head. "Damn..."

Then Callie was laughing under me, and I joined in.

Goddamn, was right.

CHAPTER TWENTY-SEVEN

CALLIE

I SAT on the edge of the tub, watching as Trevor got ready. He had on a fancy shirt and tie, with pressed slacks, and I saw the dress coat he'd be wearing them with.

My guy dressed up nice.

As for me? I was in a t-shirt of his and nothing else, sitting with my legs crossed. We were the picture of domestic and I found that I liked it.

I could get used to this.

Now, he was putting some lotion or another into his growing beard. When he'd poured the liquid in his hand, he winked at me through the mirror, telling me that he didn't need anyone else smelling me on him.

I may have turned a few shades of red.

"How long have you grown your beard before?" I asked, tipping my head.

His fingers were combing down the sides and he shrugged. "The year we won the Stanley Cup, probably. I looked like a lumber jack. Hell, we all did." He washed his hands then and when he opened his medicine cabinet to put the lotion away, I noticed...

"When were you going to tell me you have fake teeth?" He had denture stuff in the cabinet. "I mean, I guess I could pay more attention when we kiss."

He turned slowly, resting his butt against the sink as he crossed his arms over his chest.

Still, he grinned.

"I've never taken them out for you. Were you snooping?"

I shook my head.

"Did you watch a game? You watched a game on television, didn't you? When?" His smile took over his face now. "Was it last weekend? After we had our hot and heavy date?"

I shifted on the tub, uncrossing my legs, and jutted my chin up. "I didn't watch you on television."

"So, you snooped. It's cool, Callie. You're welcome to anything." His perma-smile told me he still didn't believe me.

"I watched a game on the computer. I streamed one," I admitted. "The game you got into a fight and had some amazing plus-something-or-another." I waved my hand in front of my face. "Not a big deal."

"You watched me play hockey." He pushed away from the sink, taking one slow step at a time toward me. "And that was *before* our first date. Damn." Now standing in front of me, he held out his hand and there wasn't any sense playing around; I took it and allowed him to pull me to stand.

"You look hot right now. Gorgeous." He put his hands on my sides and lowered them slowly to the bottom hem of the shirt. "Fucking beautiful."

"You're changing the subject," I said around my own smile. "Your teeth. When were you going to tell me?"

He swept his hands to my backside, his hands kneading my ass. I noticed he liked to put his hands there. Trevor was an ass guy. "Third date conversation." He started to sway us back and forth, dancing, but without any music. I put my hands to his chest, then up to his shoulders, and just went with it.

"Pretty sure we've passed third-date standards."

He shook his head. "Nope. Still gotta take you on two more proper dates."

My face widened in shock and I laughed once. "Two more dates! We've only had one date, according to you?"

"Well, yeah," he said, still swaying us. I could feel him against my stomach and if we didn't stop soon, I was going to tear him out of his very fancy clothes. "I've taken you on one *almost* proper date. Technically, it doesn't even really count. You don't sleep around on first dates." The look on his face was serious but his eyes were twinkling. "But I was coerced."

I laughed, once, again. "Coerced? Oh, no. You were very much with that program."

He shook his head. "Nope. I was debating if I was even going to go in for the kiss when I dropped you off at your door, like a gentleman."

"You were not."

"Oh, I was." He nodded a few times. "And then you pounced on me."

"I did not."

I did...

"Yeah..." His face was scrunched in faux-remorse. "Yeah, you did."

"Well, you were going to leave right after like I was just

a cheap date!" Anyone else, and they'd have taken that statement badly, but not Trevor.

"You cost me eighty dollars at Texas Roadhouse, Callie, and that wasn't even a date," he replied, around chuckles, our swaying ceasing. "You, my love, are *not* a cheap date."

My heart stopped at the endearment. Completely stopped.

But Trevor started to sway us once more, as if he didn't notice my momentary panic. "But three proper dates, Callie, and I'll take them out for you. Morning after shit."

"I've had a few morning-afters with you."

"Three proper dates."

"After the game, and maybe brunch?" I was staying over again both tonight and tomorrow night.

Saturday night, he was out of town again, so I picked up a shift at the hospital.

"That would be two more dates," I added.

"You really want to see my gummy smile, 'ey?"

I reached up, putting my hand behind his head. "I just want to see you."

"You see me," he assured me on a whisper, moments before his lips met mine in a soft kiss. "I want you to come tonight," he said, pulling back slightly. "At this rate, I don't know where I can seat you unless you sit with the wives."

"I don't..."

He rubbed his hand in circles over my back. "What's stopping you? What scares you to tell them that you're mine?" He pulled back more so he could look down at me. "Do you have some sort of hang up? What's up?" He sounded genuinely curious.

And maybe a little bit hurt.

"They all know Jenna..."

"So?"

"I'm obviously related to her."

"Again, so?"

I swallowed and fixed my eyes on his shoulder, before I said, quietly, "I've worked a long time to be someone different than my family. I'm not exactly embarrassed by them, but..." I breathed heavily and could feel the onset of tears. Stupid, stupid girly hormones. "They're going to lump me in right with her." Suddenly, my words were coming out like word-vomit. "They're going to think I'm a materialistic *bitch* and it's going to be a long three hours."

I didn't realize he'd stopped moving, nor did I realize I'd started to cry, both things that made themselves known when he put his hands on either side of my face, his thumbs brushing at the wet tracks and his face lowered and in mine. "You are nothing like Jenna, Callie. It's obvious from the moment someone meets you. Shit, Cal, you remember what you were wearing the first day I met you? Holey jeans and a tank top that you looked like you painted in. You have a 'don't care' attitude about you, but a heart the size of fucking Africa. It's in your smile, your laugh, the way you tease and joke. And I fucking love you for it."

My heart stopped again and I tried to shake my head against his hands. "You can't. It's too—"

"Too soon, yeah." He nodded. "But I'll wait for you to catch up. I have a few years on you. You're just a child, after all," he added, with a sexy wink.

My shoulders began to shake and I couldn't stop the watery laugh that bubbled out. "Hey!" I scolded, slapping at his shoulder.

He pulled me in close again and kissed my forehead. "I love you, and that's not going anywhere. You take your time."

CHAPTER TWENTY-EIGHT

CALLIE

"YOU MADE IT!" Sydney yelled as I walked into the box. She threw her hands up in the air and hurried over to me like we were really good friends, when I hardly knew the woman all that well.

I forced a smile and hugged her when she dropped her arms around my neck. "I did...!" Okay, so maybe that came off a little more forced than I intended.

Sydney lowered her voice to whisper in my ear, so none of the other women would be able to hear. "I'm very glad to see you. Trevor wouldn't let me walk you up in case you wanted to bail."

My eyes widened. "I'm so—"

She laughed and stepped back. "Oh, goodness, don't be. Let me introduce you to everyone."

I wiped my hands on my jeans. I'd told Trevor that I was going to be underdressed—I didn't have any dress-up clothes with me at his place—but he assured me that my skinny jeans and boots, with an off-the-shoulder blouse I had with me, would be fine. I didn't believe him, but apparently, he was correct.

Sydney, as team captain's wife, wore an outfit very similar, but with black leggings. The other wives had on anything from skirts, to dresses, to more jeans. I glanced around, afraid that Jenna would be here, even though Trevor reassured me that she rarely came to games.

It wasn't that I didn't want to see her, but...

I just knew how she treated her position as a hockey wife, and I didn't want her to think I was okay with the things she did.

Because I wasn't.

What little I knew about Sydney though...

My forced smile eased as I realized I could probably get along with her. She seemed easy to like.

"First, you know my boys," she said, pointing to Brandon and Brody. "The other three stayed home with a sitter. Bri likes the games, but she's a pistol in the morning if she doesn't go to bed on time. The little blond boy with my boys is Anderson Leeds. Have you met Mikey?"

I shook my head.

"You'll have to meet him. He's fun. Anderson doesn't come to many of the games, but Brandon wanted to have a play date." She shrugged then. "Sometimes you have play dates in the box." She took my elbow and moved me toward the group of five women who were up here. "This is Layla Christensen," she introduced, holding her hand out to a brunette in a skin-hugging dress. She was definitely one who made me feel out of place with her fancy clothes and made-up face. She looked like she got along with Jenna. She looked...

Layla smiled though, and waved, and I realized I was being judgmental—I was being like Jenna. I decided then to have a more open mind.

"She's married to Eric," Sydney continued. "Then we have Tasha, Nora, and Molly D." Like Layla, these women appeared kind with their smiles and hellos. "Their husbands are Alexi, Coen, and Josh, respectively. And then we have Molly A., who is actually Anderson's nanny." I smiled at the woman with dark hair. She was dressed up more than I would be if I were watching children, but I supposed she had to still fit in if she were to walk anywhere with the other women.

"I think this is all we'll have tonight. Have you heard from anyone else, Tash?"

Tasha, with brown hair and freckles on her nose, shook her head. "No. I believe the Jones kids are down with the flu." She had a slight Russian accent.

"The flu? It's May," said a blonde. Molly D.?

Tasha shrugged. "I just know what Facebook tells me."

"Anderson was over there the other day," Molly A. sighed, stuffing her hands in her jeans pockets. "I'll be plying the kid with vitamin C."

"After you're sick, vitamin C doesn't do much for you," I found myself saying. When all the women looked at me, I felt myself flushing hot. "I mean, um. I'm a pediatric nurse. Vitamins are great and all, but once you have a bug..." I shrugged. "Sorry." Totally overstepped.

Molly A.'s eyes widened, shaking her head and holding her hand out. "No, no! You're fine. Do you have suggestions?"

"If he takes vitamins, obviously keep up with them, but if he starts to show signs of the flu, just rest and water, unless he gets super sick," I answered, still a bit uneasy. Shoot; why did I open my mouth?

"I'll definitely keep an eye out. Mikey becomes a heli-copter dad when Anderson gets sick. I mean, understand-able but..."

I was curious what that meant, and why, exactly, Anderson was up here with a nanny and not his mom, but I'd save that question for Trevor. Maybe he'd know. I already felt like I said too much.

"So, you're Jenna's sister," Layla said, a thoughtful look on her face.

Everything stilled inside me, afraid of what was coming. She was my sister; I didn't want to hear shit-talk about her, but on the other side of that coin...I knew who she was. I knew how she came across.

I gave a small smile and an even smaller nod. "Yes. I am."

"You guys look alike." Layla again.

I swallowed and nodded once more. "Yeah. We do."

"And you're a nurse?" Molly D. asked.

"I am."

"For children?" Molly D.'s voice was a bit incredulous now and I could feel my heart beginning to pound.

"I am." My voice was a bit softer now, as nerves started to take root.

Thankfully, though, Sydney seemed to sense my unease. "Hey, guys, the anthem's about to begin."

Everyone, even the children, stood and I found myself impressed. We all moved toward the front and there, way down below, were the hockey teams, standing and ready to go. I tried to find Trevor, searching first the bench, then the ice, for number 32.

There he was.

The names flanking him were Prescott—Caleb—and Jones, *whose kids were sick with the flu*, I thought. The Enforcers—every single one of them—stood still for the singing of the national anthem, while the other team had a few rockers, adjusting their weight from skate to skate.

The crowd began to cheer when the singer hit "land of

the free," and sticks began to pound against the ice and walls as she eased into "...of the brave."

Soon, the men were circling and the lights were on, heavier rock music filling the air.

I found myself excited to watch the game: The energy of the arena. The sweetness of Sydney. Seeing my man on ice, looking to be smiling from ear to ear as he talked to Caleb.

And I was glad that I came.

CHAPTER TWENTY-NINE

TREVOR

THIRTY SECONDS REMAINED in Game 3 and it was currently tied—one and one. It had been a tight game, but that was to be expected in playoffs, even if it were only the First Round. Everyone was fighting to get to the next round. Everyone was hungry for their chance to hoist the Cup in just a few weeks' time.

But shit, if we didn't win tonight, it would only make the series that much more important.

I slid into the bench, stepping up to join the other D-men and, rather than popping a squat, turned to lean against the boards. No sense sitting down. Too much shit going on.

My gloved hands were braced on the wall and they were holding my weight as I watched the remaining seconds.

Dvornikov, a two-year veteran of the team, gained control of the puck.

"Let's go, let's go, let's go!" Coach murmured loudly from the back of the bench.

The ice was filled with sounds of hollers, grunts, and skates scraping the ice. Then there was the energy of the arena. The cheers were loud; Enforcers fans weren't a taunting group of the away team, but they certainly were loud supporters of us.

Dvornikov was pushed into the boards, the sound rattling all the way down here, but Bell was right there, retrieving the puck and keeping it in Enforcers' possession.

The action on the ice became harried, as the clock began to near zero.

No one liked overtime.

It was exciting, sure, but we already played sixty hard minutes. If we could get this, if we could keep possession *and* get the puck in, we were that much closer. We were only down one in the series, and we'd be amped for our game Sunday afternoon, where we'd play harder and faster.

This was just the way we rolled.

We took momentum, and we didn't slow down. Once we had a taste of victory, we were a runaway train on a downward hill. Faster, faster, faster…

Those of us on the bench began to pound on the boards, either with hands or sticks. There were murmurs among us, as we tried to plead with the hockey Gods to give us this goal.

To give us this win.

Then, in slow motion…

Bell passed the puck to Green, who lifted his stick, lowering it…

Connecting it…

"Fuck, yes!" Coach yelled, just as the crowd went crazy, simultaneous with the red light signaling the puck met net *and* the period buzzer.

Excitement rattled the arena as Texas filtered back into their bench and we ran out of ours. We tied the series. One and one.

Sure, only two games in, but shit, we had this.

I BUSTED out of the locker room, my only intentions of getting to Callie.

There, in the lounge, standing and talking to Sydney and looking like she belonged—because fuck, yes, she belonged—was my girl.

And she watched us win.

I stalked over to her, a grin on my face, even though her back was to me. Sydney caught my movement though and she grinned through whatever she was telling my girl. Before Callie could turn, I bent my knees and wrapped my arms around her middle, burying my nose into her neck.

"God, I want to bring you home," I murmured as she jumped from the shock of being surprised. I kissed her neck before grinning up at Sydney. "I'm glad you ladies are having fun, but I have things to do. *We*, have things to do."

Sydney laughed, always easy-going. "I'm sure you do... It was nice catching up, Callie. Will you be back Sunday?"

Callie looked over her shoulder at me and I just brought my brows up. That was her decision. I mean, she could stay at my apartment, naked and waiting in my bed...

Either way, I would be happy.

"I think I'll come, yes," she said, more to me than Sydney, as she was turning her head back.

"Great! If you'd like, the girls will likely get together in the morning at Hash, while the guys practice. You're welcome to join us."

I held my breath, curious if she'd take the offer. I was

good with easing Callie into this lifestyle. I wanted her to be comfortable. I wanted...

"Okay, yeah. That'd be fun."

My arms tightened around her, pleased with her decision.

"Your husband's interviewing," I interjected before they could start talking anymore, because I was sure they could, and I personally had things to do.

Things that involved Callie on her back.

Or even her stomach, with her ass in the air...

I needed her after the excitement of the game.

Fuck, I just needed her.

"Figures," Sydney answered, a slight roll to her eyes. "Comes with the name."

I chuckled and agreed, because even though I'd been an Enforcer as long as Caleb and Jonny had been, 'Enforcers' was damn near synonymous with 'Prescott,' with their father having played for the team, and the sisters slowly filtering into the front office.

Callie said her goodbyes and soon we were seated in my truck, heading back to my place.

"You guys played really well," Callie said, two, maybe three, minutes into the trip. Thank God, I lived semi-nearby, as her voice was already doing things to me.

I'd never been this amped up after a game, but something about Callie having been with me before the game, being at the game, *and* coming home with me after, had my libido all sorts of crazy.

"It was a good game," I agreed. "Only Game 3, still plenty of time for mistakes, but I think we've got this one."

"So, it's best of seven, right? So, whoever basically gets to four games won first, wins the series?"

I nodded and grinned over at her. "You were comfortable with the girls." It wasn't a question. I could hear it in the way she spoke of things she obviously had talked to them about, and in the way she walked tall beside me on the way out of the arena and to my truck.

She grinned, shifting in her seat some so she was angled toward me, her head resting against the head rest. "I was, actually. It was easy to get along with them."

"Who was there tonight?"

"Layla, the Mollys, and..." She clicked her tongue while thinking. "Oh, yes. Tasha."

"Crazy Russian," I said with a grin. "Her husband is nuts."

"She was sweet."

Nodding, I agreed. "She is. They balance each other. No...uncomfortable discussions about your sister?"

"Jenna was mentioned, but no, not really."

"Good." I reached over to take her hand in mine. "I'm glad you came."

Her smile was small but sweet. "*I'm* glad I came," she admitted quietly.

I squeezed her hand gently and turned my focus back to the drive, getting us back to my place in almost record time. "Here's how this is going to go down," I told her, helping her out of the cab.

Her face morphed into surprised shock, but she nodded. "Okay. Do tell me. How is this going down?"

I shut the truck door and walked her inside, hitting the garage button. "We're going to go straight to my room," I started, already leading her that way. "You're going to peel yourself out of those clothes, while I do the same."

"Oh, really? I thought you liked—"

To do it on my own. "Yes. Yes, I do. But I won't be held responsible for ruining your clothes."

She laughed. "Alright. Go on."

I didn't bother with the lights as we made our way

toward my bedroom. "You're going to then move to sit against the headboard, with your knees spread and your pretty pussy on display."

"Mmm. Is that so?"

"And then I'm going to make you go crazy before I slip into you. Got it?"

"And when do I get to make *you* go crazy?"

My cock jumped at that, instantly stiffening. I could feel her hands on me, her mouth on me... "Shit, not right away, baby. I'm so pumped and on edge from you being there tonight..." We entered my room and this time, I hit the lights. I loved fucking her with the lights on. I loved watching her face when she came, her pussy squeezing and milking my cock as her body reacted to mine.

"That made you happy, did it?"

"Shit, yes. Now, undress."

Her smile was wide but she did as I asked. Demanded, really. I jerked on my tie, loosening the fucker, before pulling it off over my head. She watched as I unbuttoned my shirt, even as she was removing her own clothes like a good girl.

I yanked my shirt from my trousers and pushed the fabric to the floor.

Callie was already on the bed, her legs spread like I asked.

I started on my belt, loosening it, but Callie bent the rules—she slipped her fingers between her folds.

Growling between my teeth, I forgot about my pants and moved kneel on the bed. "Do you like touching yourself?" I asked, settling between her legs.

"Mmhmm." Her finger tips moved slowly over her clit but her eyes remained locked on mine.

"Stop."

She merely lifted her brows and slid her fingers down

slowly, dipping the tips of two into herself. "Get naked, Trevor. I want to watch you jerk yourself off."

Part of me wanted to take back the control but fuck if the idea didn't turn me on.

Soon, my pants joined the heaps of clothes on the ground and I sat on my knees between Callie's feet, my hand fisting my cock.

"Do you touch yourself and think of me going down on you? My mouth on you?" I asked as I tugged on my stiff shaft.

"Yeah." Her eyes were getting heavy and she seemed to lean harder into the headboard and pillows. "And now that I've felt your beard there too, when I think of that, I get there faster." She licked her lips and dropped her eyes to where I was moving my hand. "Have you thought of me when doing that?"

"Fuck, yes," I answered hard. "All the fucking time." I squeezed a little harder, while she brought another hand down between her, angling her body so she could finger herself with one hand, and play with her clit with the other. "Fuck, Callie, that's hot. Are you going to come?"

"I'm close," she admitted, her eyes closing briefly.

"I want to watch."

"You too."

"Fuck, no."

That opened her eyes, but thankfully, did not still her hands. "Why not?"

"I'm coming in you."

"You're coming on your hand."

"Callie."

"Trevor."

"We'll stop this game," I warned, my hand slowing down. I couldn't believe we were fighting while giving ourselves hand jobs. "I'm not coming on my hand."

159

"If I come from myself, you're coming from yourself." She pushed a third finger into herself as her other hand concentrated just on her clit.

She'd make herself come.

She was probably almost there.

She bit on her lip. She was right fucking there.

I let go of my cock and reached for her hands, pulling them away from her. She laughed around her moan as I pinned her hands to her thighs and knelt in to her.

She was so fucking wet. So fucking aroused.

One lick and she'd be over that edge.

So, I did.

"Trevor!" Her body arched off the bed and her hands tightened into fists under mine.

I grasped her hips and pulled her down the bed, her back flattening and her ass lifting up as I brought her closer to my kneeling thighs. Before letting her calm down from her orgasm, I was pushing into her.

Hot. So fucking hot.

The way her pussy squeezed my hard cock, the way it took me and pushed me out. I alternated my eyes from my thrusting hips, to her tits bouncing with each hard thrust, and her face in pure ecstasy.

"Fuck, I love you," I grunted, pushing my cock against her walls again and again. I wanted to keep her high going. I didn't want her to come down.

Not yet.

But then she was bringing a hand to her clit again. "Oh, no." I grabbed her wrist, moving us so I was towering over her and had her wrists pinned against the pillow beside her head. "You're not touching yourself. Not now."

"I'm gonna..."

"Yeah. You're gonna come. From my cock. Not your hand this time. Or else I'm tying you up next time." The idea held merit, and if I wasn't already point-five seconds from shooting my load, it would have done the trick.

"It was your cock last time," she groaned, thrashing her head and squeezing her eyes shut.

"But mostly your fingers. My turn, baby. This is my turn."

"Trevor." My name was nearly an octave higher than usual and it made me smile fucking wide.

"Yeah, baby."

"I need..." Her breathing was coming out erratic.

"Yeah, you do." My thrusts were strong and sure, quickening as her breaths and moans spurred me on. It wasn't much longer before her body bowed from the bed and I didn't even bother holding back my own response—I was pulsing and shooting my cum into her within moments.

"Oh, my God," she mumbled, her eyes slowly opening.

I groaned into her ear, my body relaxing down onto hers as my hips jerked, my ass cheeks clenching. "Just Trevor," I answered. The aftereffects of her orgasm was still enough to have my cock attempt to empty itself further, but I was bone dry.

My grin against her neck was lazy.

My body lax.

My heart so fucking full.

And all because I went against my own rules, and asked to take the girl home.

Some rules were meant to be broken.

CHAPTER THIRTY

April 15

CALLIE

WHEN I WOKE, Trevor's bedroom was dark.

I glanced toward his alarm clock and saw that it was only five-twenty. I'd learned that on game days he set it for six—enough time for food, shower, and traffic, he'd told me.

Well, lucky him, I was awake early enough for a little teasing.

I smiled into the dark and looked over my shoulder. The man cuddled in his sleep; I couldn't recall a single morning where I'd slept with him, that I *didn't* wake up with my back to his chest, our legs tangled in the sheets.

It was amazing the sheets were even still on the bed.

Heck. It was amazing I was even *awake*.

I blamed Trevor for that, though. The man had my internal alarm clock going off every two hours when I was in bed with him. Again and again, throughout the night, the man woke me with his kisses.

I'd take the morning shift.

I wiggled out of his embrace and slipped from the bed, careful to not wake him. After sneaking out of the room to do morning business in the bathroom—and brushing my teeth, yes—I made my way back into his room.

Still dark, but dawn was starting to rise, casting a soft glow into the room.

He was still sleeping, though.

I held my breath and listened closely—when he was in his deepest sleep, he snored ever so lightly, even when on his side.

There it was.

Grinning, I tiptoed back to his bed but just as I stepped over his discarded clothes from the night before, words he'd said echoed in my mind, and an idea formed.

The man liked his dirty words.

And while the most he'd ever done was suck on my toes —weird, but oddly erotic—I had a feeling the man didn't mind a little kink to his sex.

I bent down to retrieve his belt and considered grabbing another, but I was afraid that too much noise rummaging around his room would wake the bear. Quietly, softly, I moved back on the bed, gently nudging him to his back after pulling the covers down. He groaned as he did, his right arm and leg dropping to his side, showing me just how relaxed his body was.

Well, his limbs anyhow, I thought, seeing his cock starting to swell as it rested on his left thigh.

The man was insatiable.

I wondered briefly how long that would last...

And then I wondered how long I *wanted* it to last...

I shook my head from thinking of forever; we were too new. There were too many outside factors to consider. I forced myself to be here and now.

Kneeling at his side, I cautiously reached for his right hand and brought it to his midline, resting his hand on his stomach, and did the same with his left. After glancing around his bed, I decided I'd have to just secure his wrists together; he had a solid wood headboard and nothing, anywhere, to secure his hands to otherwise.

Remembering the last time I woke him up like this, I couldn't help my sassy grin from popping up on my face. This time, I'd be a little slyer.

Tease a little bit more.

Last time was about feeling him against my tongue and him coming in my mouth.

I watched his face then, as I grabbed his stiffening cock and pushed it up to reset along his belly. Slowly, I dragged the tip of my finger from the bottom of his shaft, up along the vein there, to his head.

When he groaned in his sleep, I bit back a smile, before gently feathering my finger right under the head, where he was most sensitive.

Trevor's thighs bunched then his legs shifted, followed by him licking his lips in his sleep.

When his hands bunched together and the muscles in his forearms tensed, I knew he was on the verge of waking up.

"Trevor," I cooed softly, drawing my finger up and down his shaft again, twice, before teasing that sensitive spot once again.

He was hardening under my hand, the head turning deep red.

"Callie." His voice was sleep-roughened and I moved my eyes from my playing to his face, where his eyes were now open and watching me. He reached out his bound hands, trying to put them on top of my playing one.

"Keep your hands to yourself," I murmured.

"Callie..." His voice was a sexy warning this time, but his eyelids dropped closed again.

"Move your hands, Trevor." I honestly didn't think he would—I didn't think he'd give up any semblance of control, but lo and behold, he did.

"Shit, Cal," he mumbled when I began to tease him again.

"You like that?"

"Remind me to tease you later," he grunted out.

I kept playing lightly over him, my mouth watering because I wanted it on him, but more than that, I wanted to watch.

God, did I want to watch.

I straddled his thigh then, to which he wasn't shy in announcing how wet I was, but I kept up my job, loving the view of his cock hardening, swelling to its thick girth and turning deep colors.

Trevor grunted as his hips bucked. "Callie..."

"Nope."

"You don't know..."

"Just no," I said with a grin.

"God, I'm teasing you so hard later..."

I looked forward to it.

"A little more, baby," he finally said, and I felt a thrill of pleasure that I brought this out in him. That through my teasing, he was essentially begging for release. I focused my feathering fingers right to the underside of his head, flicking it back and forth.

"Shit, Cal. Fuck. Callie."

His hips were shifting and he kept rotating his legs—even the one I sat on, which only heightened my own need to come. Watching him so ready to explode, but holding back, did things to me. Like he said, I was wet and with his leg moving below me, and his cock hard and beginning to pulse ever so slightly...

His hands bunched on his stomach and I could tell he was fighting to keep them to himself, to not reach down and press my hands harder to his body.

"Sit on my cock, Cal," he finally demanded, his eyes open and drilling into mine.

I shook my head.

"No," I said. "I'm watching you come."

"Fuck, baby. No. Ride me. Hard." His hips jerked upward.

"You get to watch me come; I'm watching you."

"Yeah, when my cock is buried balls deep."

I laughed at his sassiness. Man got testy when he was on the edge.

"And when you tease me beforehand."

"I've never teased you like... Fuck, Callie." I watched as his jaw clenched.

"Just let go."

"No."

"Stubborn man."

"Gotta keep up with you," he answered between clenched teeth. "Your tongue then. Fuck, give me something."

I hummed my negative answer, then adjusted my hand so my thumb could play. My finger was getting tired.

"Shit, Callie."

"Just. Let. Go."

"No."

"Okay."

And then I stood from the bed.

Turned away.

"Fuck, Callie, come back here." His words were rushed and...pained.

The man had the ability to stand, just as he had the ability to move his hands, but he lay there, his eyes open and heavy with heat and want, as his cock throbbing and swaying up toward his stomach.

As fun as this had been, suddenly I was having visions of finishing him off in the shower.

"No," I finally said, before saucily turning and heading toward the bathroom.

He'd follow me.

Of that, I was absolutely certain.

CHAPTER THIRTY-ONE

TREVOR

SHE DID NOT JUST...

But sure shit, she did.

I watched as Callie walked, bare-assed naked, into the bathroom.

I scrambled to sit, flipping my feet off the bed as I brought my belt-bound wrists to my mouth, using my teeth to work my hands free.

I walked heavily toward the bathroom, my hands eventually rubbing at my wrists to work out any kinks, and watched as she grinned over her shoulder at me, stepping into the glass-enclosed shower.

I'd much rather be in the tub with her but...

Regardless of where she was going, I wasn't far behind.

In the confines of the shower, I cornered her. I didn't bother with niceties. Not with small talk.

No, I just pushed her against the wall and slammed my mouth to hers. One hand on her face, the other slipping behind her back, pulling her body tight against my painfully hard cock.

"You tease," I mumbled against her mouth.

She licked along the inside of my mouth but then brought her hands to my chest and pushed back, turning us so my back was to the cold tile.

Before I could protest, her hands were grasping my cock and she was working me.

Shit, I was almost there already; she had very little to do before my balls were tightening.

"Dammit, Callie," I groaned, fighting to hold back.

"Why are you fighting it?" she asked. "Just let go, Trevor. Let it go." Then she grinned and said it again, in a sing-song voice.

I couldn't focus on holding myself back then; I was too busy laughing at Callie, but my laugh quickly turned to a grunt as I released up and toward my stomach, my cum also falling down to coat her hand.

"God, Callie," I groaned, my shoulders slagging against the wall.

It was going to take me a few minutes to recover but dammit, I was going to, because I needed her. I need her heat. I needed her tightness. I needed...

She licked her way over my stomach, lapping up my cum and like that, I was ready to fucking go again.

"God, I'm too old for this," I mumbled, my balls already impossibly tight. "I'm going to tease you later. Right now, I'm in you." My cock was ready; my body was still a few minutes behind, but no matter. I managed to turn her and bend her, so her hands braced against a seated ledge, her ass in the air.

I wasted no time and was in her quickly, pulling her hips back to mine and thrusting hard, deep, as she moved against me with just the same amount of enthusiasm.

Her moans and words echoed in the shower, the sound of the falling water only enhancing the sights, the sounds. I watched as water fell down her back, all the while, I was pounding into her and grunting, her ass shaking each time our bodies met.

In record time, I was coming again, just as she did the same.

Best.

Morning.

Ever.

CHAPTER THIRTY-TWO

May 5

CALLIE

"I'LL GET BACK to you on our decision. I do think you would do wonderful with our company."

I smiled into my laptop camera. "Thank you so much, Kim. I look forward to hearing back from you."

After pleasantries were exchanged, the signal cut out and I sighed heavily, resting back into the chair I sat on in the kitchen.

I closed my eyes, thinking about the interview with the travel nursing company, and smiled. I had the job. I just knew it.

I opened my eyes to my quiet kitchen, my gaze landing on my phone just as the time flashed.

Trevor had been out of town for hockey and was due home later tonight.

You're going to have to tell him.

My smile slowly faded.

The last few weeks had been phenomenal. I absolutely loved spending time with Trevor and although he didn't say it often, I could feel that he meant it when he said he loved me.

But what did that mean with my plans?

Hell, the man didn't even know I'd been *looking* to leave California.

And now, there was a very real possibility of it happening.

I was going to have to come clean.

Maybe we weren't meant to last.

Maybe he told every girl he slept with, he loved them.

Maybe I was just another number.

Maybe...maybe...maybe...

Shit, this was going to hurt him.

I closed my laptop then and pinched the bridge of my nose. What was I going to do? I enjoyed being with Trevor, but I wanted this opportunity. *So. Badly.*

So, so badly.

I was only twenty-two. This was my time.

My time to travel, to grow, to find myself.

Then why did I feel the most found when I was with Trevor? Was he worth giving up my dreams?

Honestly? No.

No person was worth giving up a piece of yourself.

But maybe...

I could always take assignments nearby. Maybe take farther ones during the hockey season. Perhaps I could...

And there I went, thinking about the future. I didn't even know what the future held, when it came to Trevor.

Every time we were together, it was sex. We had a healthy sexual relationship.

Was that all we had?

I dropped my hands to my lap and sighed. I had big

decisions to make, and I'd have to make them soon. There was no sense keeping this up with Trevor if I wasn't planning on sticking around.

My phone buzzed against the table with an incoming text. I tapped the screen, only to see it was from Jenna.

Wanting money.

I should tell her *no*. I should tell her that if she wanted to book such a ridiculously expensive trip without talking to me about it first, she had to foot the entire bill.

But I also knew what a dinner in the MacTavish house was like, when Jenna had an issue with something you've said or did to her, and we were due a family meal sooner than later.

Quite honestly? I didn't want to deal with it.

If I was offered one of these travel nursing positions, I'd make up the hit to my savings. Next time, Jenna wouldn't get away with it, though.

I was opening my banking app to just be done with this trip, when a knock on the door broke the otherwise silence of my apartment. Frowning, I stood from the table and moved to check it. I wasn't expecting anyone...

On the other side, stood Trevor.

My first reaction was absolute thrill, as was evident by the fact I was soon all around him, arms and legs wrapped as I hugged him tight.

He laughed as he stepped us back into my apartment, closing the door behind him. "Why, hello."

"You're home! I thought you weren't coming in until tomorrow?" I leaned back, but kept my limbs wrapped around him. It was amazing what a few days away from him did to me.

This relationship was still fairly new, but *God,* I enjoyed being with him...which made my upcoming decision that much harder.

"We were able to get our charter out sooner." His grin was wide as he leaned in to kiss me once, before lowering me to the ground. As I stepped back, he lifted his brows. "You're all dressed up. You have a hot date?" His voice was teasing, but I could still hear the curiosity.

I wasn't ready to tell him.

I had to come up with a plan...

My heart squeezed in my chest because I knew I couldn't keep it from him. "I had an interview."

"An interview?" He frowned and I took his hand, pulling him toward the couch. "I thought you liked your job."

"I do. I do..." I pushed him to sit before moving to take a seat beside him, my leg up on the couch between us as I faced him. "I, um..."

I scrunched my face, looking around.

"Callie..."

Better to get it over with.

"One of the things I liked most about the missionary work, was the traveling," I started, slowly. "And at work a few weeks ago, someone was speaking highly about travel nursing." I forced my eyes back to his, trying to gauge his reaction.

"What is that, exactly?" he asked. He didn't look upset or put out, but rather, curious.

"You take contracts with different hospitals and clinics, for different lengths of time. You could have an assignment in LA, and then later, take one in, I don't know... Massachusetts, if you really wanted."

He frowned then. "So, you're leaving?"

I didn't think three words could ever devastate me so much. He had a very strong, stoic look to his face, but his words spoke volumes otherwise.

I rushed to reassure him. "No, no. Not necessarily. It was just an interview. I don't know anything..."

"But you want to leave."

"I..."

He nodded, and the action alone cut off my ability to speak. I wanted to say I was sorry, but I didn't know what I was apologizing for.

When he stood though, I quickly followed. "Trevor."

He just shook his head, walking backward toward the door as his eyes remained on my face. "Just... I need a minute."

He turned then, leaving me with my mouth gaping open, but no words to tell him to get him to stay.

And just like that, he was gone.

CHAPTER THIRTY-THREE

TREVOR

THIS DAY HAD GONE *to hell and back, really fucking quickly,* I thought as I sat on my couch, nursing a beer.

The team got back, we were heading into a seven-day break thanks to a quick series, and the very first person I wanted to see dropped a bombshell on me.

She was fucking leaving.

Callie was fucking going.

What the hell did I do in a previous life, to not be someone women wanted for good. And the real shitter was, what I had with Callie was so fucking perfect. So much better than any woman I'd been with before.

I took a chance on her. I broke all my rules with her.

And I thought it ended up being a good thing.

But now she was fucking moving.

Then, to top it all the fuck off, Marlo called me, said she was basically considering getting back with Jordan, only for the fucker to call me, asking to come and chat. He came, he talked, he left—without a shiny new black eye to commemorate the moment, but that had been close.

Fucker.

I had enough things to worry about than their marital issues.

They were fucking divorced.

For a reason!

I could be Marlo's sound board. If she wanted support and someone by her side, I could be that person, but I didn't necessarily agree with her and Jordan getting back together. The fucker screwed up, not just five years ago, not every year since, but again tonight.

The two of them would do whatever the hell they wanted, but I wasn't about to watch that shit show explode again.

My phone beeped and I picked it up.

Callie's name flashed and for the briefest of moments, I considered deleting the message, unread.

I thought about my friends' confessions of miscommunication.

This wasn't miscommunication. This was simply not *communicating.*

Callie's decision to look into traveling was not a decision she made at the spur of the moment. For her to have had an interview today, that meant this was something she'd been thinking about for a while.

Even likely as long as she and I had been together.

My phone beeped again but I ignored it, tossing back the last of my beer and standing to head to the kitchen.

As I left the kitchen, my phone began ringing from the couch.

She was persistent.

And I was fucking hurt.

I'd deal with it in the morning, I thought, ignoring my phone and heading to my room.

My room that smelled like her.

Fuck.

It was going to be a long fucking night.

BAM, *bam, bam.*

The sound of someone pounding on my door had my glazed-over eyes focusing in the dark room.

The knock sounded again.

Who the hell was here at... I glanced at the clock.

Eleven at night.

Shit.

I could have ignored it, but the knocking continued, making it hard to not notice. I found myself getting out of bed and tugging up my jeans as I walked to the front. "I'm coming," I mumbled.

When I pulled open the door, I was honestly shocked that the pounding from the other side came from little Callie MacTavish.

Gone were her fancy interview clothes, and instead, she showed up here in shorts and hoodie, looking every bit the laid-back, easy Callie that I thought I knew.

Fool's me.

"What, you don't answer your phone anymore?" she asked, before pushing herself inside, not bothering to wait to be let in.

"When someone doesn't answer, it usually means they don't feel like talking," I said, shutting the door behind her.

She turned on me, anger emitting from her tiny body. "Yeah, well, you said you needed a minute—about *seven hundred of them* ago."

"Slight exaggeration."

"You're a pissy girl when you don't get your way, you know that?" She moved to stand toe to toe with me. "When you're upset about something, you *talk* about it. Especially if it's with someone you allegedly love." She put her hands to my bare chest and had the audacity to shove me.

And I let her.

Once.

She rounded on me again, looking to do it again, but I wasn't about to let her a second time. "Yeah, well, when someone says they love the other, they expect a certain amount of respect, and part of that includes knowing when the hell their significant other is planning on bailing," I said, catching her hands to me, trapping her wrists in my hands and prying her off.

"I wasn't *bailing*," she said between gritted teeth.

"What the hell do you think it sounds like, to be told you were interviewing to fucking leave? Huh, Callie? What does that sound like?"

She pinched her lips together tightly, her eyes never wavering from mine, as she said, "I hadn't made a decision."

"But you started the fucking process. When? When did you start? Before we met? Right after? Shit, Cal, it had to be at least two weeks ago! We've been together for nearly every fucking day for six weeks!"

"Yeah, Trevor, six weeks. A month and a half! That's not enough time to start declaring undying love and affection."

I shook my head, dropping her hands from mine and stepping around her. "Yeah, well. When you know, you know."

"How many girls have you told you loved them, huh, Trevor?" she yelled at my retreating back. "You said it *four-*

teen days in! Guys who do that generally don't hold weight to those three words."

I turned and was on her so quickly, I don't think she was expecting it. "Not fucking once," I spoke down to her, keeping my hands fisted at my sides. "Not. Fucking. Once." Maybe in high school, but... "I'm a thirty-two-fucking-year old man, Callie. I know what I want and when I want it. I know myself pretty damn well by this point. I knew better than to get mixed up in something with someone so young. But I liked being with you. You showed your maturity in the things you said, the things you did, the way you lived your life, but apparently I was still looking at it all with rose-colored glasses because you're not as damn grown up as I thought you were."

"That's not fair!" she yelled after me, after I turned away from her again.

"What's not fair is finding out you're planning on leaving. What's not fair, is thinking we were on the same page," I said, stalking toward the kitchen. Fuck, I needed another drink.

"Well, then, we *talk about it*!" she yelled. "We don't walk away in a tiff."

The fact that she was talking to me like I was in the wrong... My chuckle was dry and unamused.

As badly as I wanted alcohol, I settled for water. Being hungover before practice tomorrow wouldn't be my best idea.

"Then frickin' talk," I said when she entered the kitchen area. "This information is like a fucking one-eighty, Callie." I lifted the glass of water to my mouth as Callie stood nearby, her arms crossed over her chest.

"Yes, I put in the applications after we started seeing each other. Yes, I should have told you about it, but I honestly didn't think anything of it. Most of these companies want experience and quite honestly, I don't have a ton of it. Not in a hospital sense," she started, her eyes never leaving my face. I braced my hands on the counter in front of me and made myself listen. "I forgot about it. Every now and then, I'd remember, but until I knew it was a possibility, why would I put that wrench there? I like being with you, Trevor. You make me really freaking happy." Her voice cracked and I could tell she was going to cry.

So much for making her happy.

"But what? I put my future on hold because *maybe* a guy wants to be with me?"

"What part of *I love you* says that 'maybe' I want to be with you?" I gripped the counter harder.

She shrugged and blinked, the first tear falling.

I'm going to stay strong. I will stay strong.

"Trevor, you're an athlete. And not just a weekend, just-for-fun one, but the real deal. I've spent years fighting from being this kind of person, the one living in the spotlight. I want to be a normal, average girl, and being with you doesn't allow that. But more than that... You're a professional *athlete*."

"So you said."

"You're gone all the time. You have available women in any city."

"Are you shitting me right now?" She did not just basically tell me she thought I whored around when I left San Diego.

Callie pressed on though. "And I've watched my sister and Jonny. Your profession isn't one for happy marriages."

I wasn't letting her continue down this path. I pushed from the counter but remained where I was. "One, Jonny and Jenna aren't happy, because Jenna's a bitch. Sorry, not sorry. Two, the fact you'd even consider for a minute that I'd *look* at another woman while I'm with you, is fucking absurd. Three... So, I'm gone a few nights a month. You work at least two nights every *week*. What's the fucking difference? Should I be jealous of the hot doctors you work with?" I asked, intentionally being incredulous. "What about those EMT guys? I've watched medical dramas. You're all having orgies in the available patient rooms, if those shows are to be believed."

"I would never—"

"And I wouldn't ever, to you, either. Give a guy some credit, Callie." I shook my head and muttered, "Jesus."

She stared at me a moment longer, silent tears still dropping every few seconds. *Stay strong, Trevor*, I told myself again, when all I really wanted to do was pull her close and convince her I wasn't the one going anywhere.

"Okay. I guess..." She shook her head, no longer looking pissed but rather, resigned. "We'll talk tomorrow, I guess."

Where the hell did she think she was going? "You are not fucking driving at this hour, like that," I told her, moving toward her now-retreating back.

"Well what do you propose I do?" Her sass was back.

I shook my head. "Just... come to bed. We'll figure everything out in the morning."

"We're fighting, Trevor! I'm not going to bed with you."

I stepped close, giving in to my desire to cup her face and tip her head back. Yeah, I was still pissed. Still hurt.

But I also still loved the woman.

"Come to bed," I repeated slowly, my voice low. "We'll figure it out in the morning."

I could feel her clench her jaw under my palms, but thankfully, she didn't argue.

THIRTY MINUTES LATER, both of us on separate sides of the bed, I looked over at her, only to see her staring at the ceiling, much as I had been.

"Talk to me about this gig," I finally said.

She rolled her head on the pillow to look at me, before looking back at the ceiling and pulling the sheet up to her chin, well over the shirt of mine she'd put on before climbing into bed with me.

I turned to my side, facing her. I hated this distance. "Talk to me, Cal," I whispered.

"I'm sorry." Her voice was soft, and cracked into the quiet darkness. Even in the dark, I could see as another tear slipped down her cheek and into her hairline.

I scooted over in the bed, pulling her to me now. I was through with the distance. We had our fight; it was time to move past it. "What does this job entail, if you were to get it?" I asked, ignoring her apology. "Short time away? Long time away? Tell me about it."

She was quiet for a while and I was convinced she wasn't going to tell me—and that if she wasn't going to tell me, this was definitely the start of the end of us—but eventually she said, "Contracts vary in length. And in location."

"Do you get a say?"

She nodded before dropping her face to look at me. "Yeah."

"Did you know," I started, putting my hand on her stomach, "Alexi and Tasha—you remember her, right?" When she nodded, I continued, "He was stateside for nearly a year before she made it over. As long as you promise to come home every few weeks..." I shrugged into the dark. "I think I can be strong enough to give you this. And hell, maybe even during the summer, we'll live wherever you're at."

183

"Some of the contracts are months long," she whispered in the dark.

That'd be a hell of a long time... "I'd obviously prefer the shorter ones," I admitted, allowing a small smile to cross my face, "but it's a bridge I'd be okay crossing if we got to it. Okay? Just...talk to me about it."

I heard as she swallowed hard, before she nodded. Her heavy sigh was wet, but relieving. "Okay."

CHAPTER THIRTY-FOUR

August 19
Current Year

TREVOR

SOMEHOW, Callie and I managed to make it a year. Shit, not somehow, because I knew how. I loved the hell out of that girl. It had taken a few months, but eventually she started saying it too, and now, a year later, we officially lived together.

Last year, the Enforcers won the Cup; unfortunately, this year it wasn't meant to be. Comically, though, it was the youngest Prescott that got to hoist it above his head.

Callie and I sat at home, watching the game, where she confessed she didn't know the youngest Prescott that well. I was more than happy to share with her stories that I'd been told through the years.

These days, Callie and I were good as gold, past arguments not necessarily forgotten about, but the hurts were definitely healed. Or so I'd thought.

It was somewhere around our year anniversary when negative things started to nudge their way to the surface.

First, there was a night we did dinner with her parents. The elder MacTavishes talked about a vacation they'd gone on the previous winter, while Callie slowly shook her head in their direction, panic on her face, as if she didn't realize I could see it.

When I asked about it on the way home, she said it was nothing.

Strike one.

I knew my girl well enough to know it was something, but I let her have it. We were good otherwise, so why would I purposely bring up something that apparently had the power to drive us apart. However, it wasn't the only thing of late that had me questioning what we'd built over the months.

Her laptop was open at the kitchen counter the other night, too, a spreadsheet of possible assignments she was interested in maximized on the screen. She'd been with the travel company for the last eight months, and up until this point, had been taking assignments within a four-hour-drive radius of San Diego, usually nothing more than six weeks.

But this list...

This list had my heart stopping.

Number one on her list of places for her next assignment?

A four-month stint in New York.

She'd never mentioned it.

Strike two.

The last thing shouldn't have bothered me. It shouldn't have accounted for a strike against my growing panic, but it just proved that as close as we were, she still held things back from me.

A year into our relationship, and she still held things back...

I was standing at the kitchen counter, cutting up potatoes for a roast—by Callie's direction—when her phone buzzed from the charging dock we'd placed there.

The screen lit up, the text message preview telling me more than enough:

Jenna: You owe me five thousand Callie. I need it yesterday.

"Hey, Cal?" I called out, frowning. I tried to remind myself that Callie's money was her money. She could spend it as she wished. But it was the fact she didn't talk to me about it...

Why did Callie owe Jenna so much money? We didn't ever really talk about money, other than when bills came up. I paid the mortgage and she insisted on paying utilities— which we got into a fight about initially, but I eventually caved, because some things just weren't worth the fight.

"What's up?" Callie asked, walking into the kitchen.

I chopped the current potato into eight large chunks before saying, "Jenna texted you."

She turned her head, frowning. "Okay?"

Obviously, it wasn't a rare occurrence to hear from a family member, but, "Your phone lit up. I didn't...open it..." God, why did I feel like I was the one in the wrong here? *It's her money*, I reminded myself. But shit, five thousand dollars?

If anything, her frown deepened and she walked over, reaching for her phone.

Just as she opened the screen, I asked, "Why do you owe her so much money? I mean, if you're hurting for money, I wish you would have said something. I don't care what you've done with yours or whatever, but..."

She blew out a heavy breath, a mumbled *fuck* coming out of her mouth.

Shit. This didn't sound promising.

CHAPTER THIRTY-FIVE

C̶ALLIE

FUCK ME.

I shook my head to myself, not sure how to answer him.

It's not a big deal, I tried convincing myself, but really...

Hardly a month had passed since Jonny asked Jenna for a divorce. Jenna was coming back for the trip money because the divorce drained her account; of that, I had no doubt. She tried wringing Jonny dry—not that that surprised me—and now she was likely near bankrupt, at least to Jenna standards.

"It's not a big deal," I finally told Trevor, as I went into my banking app. I swore I'd done this already...but then remembered that no, no I hadn't.

I was actually surprised Jenna let it go this long without trying harder for it.

I rubbed a hand over my face roughly and I quickly worked on sending the money over.

The thing was, though...

Trevor just days ago said we should go on a trip, and I

told him I didn't want to spend that kind of money on an exotic trip. We didn't need to.

I took a few weeks off between assignments and we'd done a few bed-and-breakfast things, but I didn't *need* to go anywhere fancy with Trevor. I liked being here with him when I wasn't working.

He nodded, and I could sense that he wanted to ask. For the last year, we'd been pretty good and open in our relationship when it came to communication. The fact he was holding back...I knew it was a bigger deal than I hoped it would be.

After sending the money, I looked up to see him back to cutting potatoes, tossing them into the roast pan where everything else was set up and ready to go.

His movements were jerky.

I got the distinct feeling that he was pissed.

"Trevor, it's not a big deal."

He shrugged, shaking his head once, but didn't look at me. "You keep your secrets, Callie," he finally said, looking up at me before tossing his cutting board and knife in the sink.

"What's that mean?" I frowned, feeling my own rising discontent. "Do you have something to say? Let's be honest, Trevor. Isn't that your policy? Let's *talk about it*?" I wasn't being fair. I knew it. I knew I was in the wrong, but...

"Nope, that's yours." He glanced at me before turning on the sink to wash his hands. "Why do you owe Jenna money?" After drying his hands on a towel, he tossed it on the counter before leaning back, his arms crossed over his broad chest.

"A trip for our parents," I ground out.

"Five thousand dollars? Did you fund the entire thing?" His voice was raised.

"It was half," I admitted, looking away. It was no secret

190

that my family spent big bucks on extravagant things, but it still had a way of embarrassing the hell out of me.

"Ten thousand fucking dollars for a trip? That you didn't go on?"

I clenched my jaw and stared at him across the kitchen, crossing my own arms. "And you just handed that over to her, no big deal, but won't take a one-K vacation with me?"

"I was trying to put it off. Shit. I did put it off," I admitted. "But the divorce put a wrench in that plan."

"Just like you were putting off telling me that you wanted to take a job in New York." He said it so coolly, I had to replay the words in my head to be sure I heard him correctly.

"Excuse me?"

"I saw your list, Cal. Not one of your top prospects for your next assignment was anywhere *near* California. What happened to talking about it? About taking the further out, longer trips during the off-season? You know damn well that things will start moving again in a few weeks."

"Were you *snooping*?!" I dropped my arms to my sides.

"No, it was open. Just like your damn phone was here, telling me you owed your sister thousands of dollars."

"I didn't accept the assignment." God, how I wanted to. I wanted to experience the city, just for a few months. Just to say I could, that I did it. And while, yeah, it was a longer assignment, I never said I was staying away. That particular one would have had me back in California by Christmas...

Which I fully intended on coming back for.

Trevor was here.

But God, how I wanted to accept the assignment.

"That's your answer? You didn't accept it?"

"What else do you want me to say, Trevor?"

"I want you to stay here!" Even from my side of the kitchen, I could see his body trembling with anger, and all it

191

was doing was fueling my own temper. "I want you to be comfortable living *here*. Why the hell do you have to leave?"

"Because I want to!"

Wrong answer, MacTavish...

I sucked in a breath as the air around us stilled.

After a moment of silence, he finally nodded. "Got it. Loud and clear."

I TOSSED the uncooked roast in the garbage after Trevor didn't come back an hour later.

When he still wasn't back an hour after that, my emotions were overruling everything.

He wanted to storm out of here without a word?

Fine.

He wanted to fight and get pissed, then not bother coming back to 'talk it out,' like he swore we would do if this type of thing came up?

Fine.

I knew better than to do things in the heat of the moment.

I knew better, but still, I did it.

I accepted the New York position.

CHAPTER THIRTY-SIX

August 23

TREVOR

"YOU KNOW," Caleb told me as we sat at the beach of their family lake house. I didn't come out here with them often, I think this was only my third or fourth time, but I'd needed to get away, and Caleb, Sydney, and the kids had been heading to Wisconsin early to open the house before the rest of the family arrived.

So, I hitched a ride with them.

I wasn't normally so spontaneous but fuck if everything crumbling with Callie didn't make me do stupid shit.

I was officially done with relationships. I wasn't good at them, apparently. Even though I managed to be really damn good at this one for a record sixteen months.

"For all your bitching last year about Jordan and Marlo," Caleb continued, "you're sure acting like him. When's the last time you talked to Callie?"

I ground my molars together but didn't answer. I didn't

appreciate being compared to Jordan Byrd, even if he and Marlo *were* allegedly—fuck, no alleged to it; they were—happy right now.

"I thought she made you happy."

"She does," I answered automatically.

"Then why the heck are you here, and not there?"

"It's complicated."

Caleb grunted and stood, dropping my phone to my lap. "Then fucking uncomplicate it. Preferably before the season. You're being salty, and I'll be damned if I'm playing with your ass in this mood."

"You don't get a choice on the team," I told him, not bothering to pick up my phone.

"Nice comeback." Caleb began to walk away. "Call your girl."

I was pissed.

I was hurt.

Why the fuck didn't she talk to me?

I looked down at my phone; Callie's missed calls, voice mails, and text messages being the only numbers to flash across the screen.

Shit, I was so pulling a Byrd right now.

Fuck.

Resigned, I stood and opened my call screen.

I stared out at the lake as the phone rang in my ear. Waiting...

"Hello?" Her voice was soft.

"Callie, baby." I took a deep breath, a rush of emotions flowing through me. Shit, I'd been stupid to leave. "I'm sorry."

She didn't say anything, not that I expected her to.

"I shouldn't have stormed out. I should have stayed and talked about it."

When she remained quiet, I basically began pleading

with her. "I love you, Cal. Please don't... Shit, Callie. I'm coming home. Please don't go anywhere."

I wasn't sure she'd answer, but quietly, her, "I'll be here," filtered through the line.

I didn't get back home for nearly twenty hours, thanks to planes and layovers—which allowed for some expensive shopping, because fuck if I was letting her go again—but the moment I pushed opened the door to our place, Callie was in my arms.

Home.

No more stupid shit.

Never again.

CHAPTER THIRTY-SEVEN

August 24

CALLIE

HE WAS GOING to kill me.

Or really, I was going to kill him.

As soon as he found out, he would be devastated.

I didn't want to think about it. So, I chose not to.

I chose to love Trevor with all I had, be with him as if we hadn't made stupid decisions in the heat of the moment; that we hadn't had one hell of a fight that had him leaving for a week and me making a stupid, stupid decision. One that I couldn't take back.

After one of the best love-making moments we had, I knew I couldn't hold it back any longer. I knew I had to tell him.

My mind was racing as Trevor stood in the shower with me, his hands running through my hair like the last week hadn't happened.

I had to tell him...

I looked up at him, panic beginning to set.

"What's up, Cal?" he asked, and I could hear...shit, I could hear the uncertainty in his voice.

My heart was pounding.

I couldn't breathe.

I looked at his eyes, knowing that by not saying anything, I was scaring him, but I didn't know how to say it. I didn't know how to ease into it.

I didn't know...

"I'm taking the job," I blurted.

His face paled. "You're taking the job," he repeated slowly.

I fought to swallow past the lump in my throat. God *damn,* this was hard.

"Really, Cal?" His voice was so soft, I almost couldn't hear it over the shower. I couldn't manage any words over the need to vomit. Oh, my God, this was killing me. Why? Why did I do it? I always let emotion overrule. I should have known he'd be back, that we could work through it.

Why did I accept it?

"God, Cal, give me something here."

My eyes burned and I shook my head, fighting to swallow past that damn lump again. "I'm sorry. God, Trevor, I'm so sorry."

"Fuck," he mumbled, and I jumped when his fist connected with the tile.

"Trevor."

"Fuck, Callie." His voice was breaking and I swear I could see a sheen of tears in his eyes. "Why?"

I couldn't say it was an accident, because it wasn't. It was intentional.

"I was hurting, Trevor," I whispered.

"So, you thought it would be a great idea to lash out like that?"

"I'm sorry," I said again, not sure what else I could say.

Trevor tipped his head back and I sucked my lips into my mouth, biting down on them. I wanted to touch him, to hold him...

"I shouldn't ask this. Fuck, you said how badly you wanted it." He was mumbling to the ceiling but lowered his face again to look at me. "There's no way you can cancel it, can you? God, Callie, I hate that I'm asking that but, shit..."

I shook my head. I'd electronically signed the contract.

"How long?"

"Sixteen weeks," I whispered, confirming what he likely knew.

Trevor nodded a few times, looking everywhere in the shower but at me. "When do you leave?"

I had a hard time getting the words out. My heart was breaking as I could see his own shatter. Why did I do it? Why? "The thirtieth," I finally managed.

I watched as his throat worked through his own swallow, as his body trembled...as he looked everywhere by me.

That was the part that hurt me the most.

He finally looked at me, but his words...

God, his words told me just how hurt he was. "Was tonight a goodbye fuck then?"

My eyes burned again; this time, there was no stopping the tears as I shook my head. "No."

"What was it then, Callie? I come home and it was like forgiveness and happiness, and then you drop this on me? What is it?"

"Trevor..." I didn't know what to do. I didn't know how to fix this.

He shook his head, no longer looking at me again. "I can't do this right now," he said before turning his back and pushing through the glass door.

"Trevor." He grabbed a towel, wrapping it around his

hips, and headed for the door. "Trevor!" I fumbled with the water before storming out after him, grabbing a towel and wrapping it around me as I followed behind quickly.

He wasn't in our room. He wasn't in the hall.

I found him in the kitchen, standing against the island with his hands braced, his head hanging low.

"Trevor."

He looked up then, the hurt written all over his face.

"Trevor," I said again, softly.

"I want forever with you, Callie," he admitted, almost as softly. "But I'm terrified that I'm going to let you go, that you're going to go to New York, and then decide to do another assignment somewhere that's not California. I can't sit here, hoping you're going to come home." He sounded like he was breaking up with me.

"Please don't do this," I pleaded.

"It's better to do it now, than to do it months down the road, don't you think?" He was breaking up with me. But even though I could see this wasn't easy for him, it was tearing me apart. "Holding out, hoping that you'll come home?"

"I'll come home."

"But what if you don't?"

I shook my head, walking up to him. "I'll come home."

He closed his eyes from me and my heart broke—it shattered—when a tear slipped down his face. "I can't hold you back, Cal." He opened his eyes again; the whites were red. "I've known for the last year that this traveling thing is what you wanted. I should have walked away back then. I should have—"

I grabbed his face, and pulled his mouth to mine. I didn't want to hear words of walking away. Words of moving apart instead of together.

Words that proved he loved me, but loved me enough to let me go.

We cried as we kissed. I felt his tears mixing with mine, falling over my hands. As they tended to do, our kisses eventually turned heated, and we moved from standing in the kitchen, to laying in our bed.

Tonight, we made love slowly.

Sweetly.

I could hear his echo of goodbye.

I didn't want goodbye.

No.

...never goodbye.

CHAPTER THIRTY-EIGHT

August 25

TREVOR

I WOKE up to an empty bed, to an alarm I didn't remember setting.

My first thought was that she left. Callie left. She was gone. She wasn't coming back...

But then I realized...

Where would she have gone?

I listened hard, hoping to hear movement in the house but came up with nothing.

I pushed myself up to sit and ran my palms against my face roughly. The last twelve hours...shit, this fucking month...was a test in patience.

Callie was going to be leaving me.

I had to get that through this heart of mine.

I dropped my hands to the bed beside me, thinking about the ring that was hanging out in my carry-on luggage.

Good thing I insured it.

Sighing, I moved to get out of the bed, but my hand met paper. Frowning, I turned my head, seeing a sheet of loose leaf. I picked it up, curious.

I'd like for you to meet me at the airport at eight. You don't have to bring anything, just your sunny disposition. Leave your worries at home. But if I don't see you there, I'll understand.

There were some crossed out words, words that her pen didn't cover enough so she went over and blackened them out with a Sharpie, as well.

At the bottom, she finished: *I'm sorry. I love you. I hope to see you.*

I glanced at the alarm clock, realizing it had been set intentionally. I had an hour and a half to meet her.

...if I don't see you, she'd said.

If all I had were five more days with her...

Shit, I was taking them.

CHAPTER THIRTY-NINE

CALLIE

I STOOD OUTSIDE OF SECURITY, tapping my phone against my hand.

He had to come. He had to be coming...

I glanced over at the clock hanging on a far wall, then back at the line for security. If he wasn't here in the next two minutes, I'd either have to head home with my tail between my legs, or get on the plane by myself.

Please be coming. God, please be on your way, Trevor.

I glanced at the line again nervously. I didn't have much time. The line was getting longer by the second and I was already cutting it close to making it to the gate on time.

I chewed on my cheek, a feeling of dread finally settling over me.

He's not coming.

He wasn't coming.

I'd hurt him that badly.

He wasn't coming.

The money was spent. *It's just money.* But I didn't want

to spend time in our place; not if he was going to be there and ignoring me.

Mind reluctantly made up, I left my place and headed toward the security line. I'd checked everything but my purse so I, myself, would make it through quickly enough. It was the throng of people in front of me that had the ability to slow this down.

A child in front of me smiled at me, showing off a toothless gap.

Trevor teased me with his toothless smile once or twice. The thought had me smiling sadly at the child.

Soon, though, I found myself stifling a sob that was fighting to tear its way through.

I sniffed, throwing my shoulders back and fighting to forget it, and moved with the line, glancing at my phone. I hoped I got to the gate on time.

There was a hustle behind me, but I was busy pulling out my license; I was only a few people away from the TSA agent.

"Excuse me. Pardon me. Yeah. Sorry. Excuse me."

Someone was persistent. I shook my head at the rudeness of some people. There were lines for a reason. You didn't just show up late.

"Yeah, yeah, I am," I heard. "I have to... Sorry. After security. Yeah. Sure. Sorry. I have to..."

Frowning, I looked over my shoulder, just as the intruder called loudly, "Callie!"

My heart stopped at the very moment my eyes locked with Trevor's.

He was here.

He made it.

He pushed past the next person in line, and didn't even give me a moment to register he was here; he simply grabbed my face and kissed me hard.

I squeezed my eyes tight, the tears I'd fought to keep away fighting to come to the surface now. Every bad feeling in my body, eased with this simple kiss.

There was a tap on my shoulder. "Ma'am."

Trevor pulled back, grinning down at me.

"You made it," I said, then shook my head as I realized the tap was because the agent was waiting for us. I fumbled with my phone, pulling up the tickets on my airline app.

I handed over my phone and my license. "Both of our tickets are there," I mumbled.

Trevor handed over his own license, his other hand resting on my back.

I couldn't believe...

He'd made it.

I glanced up at him, and he smiled down at me.

My phone and our licenses were handed back and we were ushered through the rest of security. After our shoes were put on, I finally took the hug I'd wanted.

"I can't believe you're here," I mumbled into his chest as he hugged me back, just as tightly.

"I want all the time I can get with you," he whispered into my hair, squeezing me a little bit tighter. "So." He pulled back, squeezing my hand. "Where are we headed?"

Before I could open my mouth, the overhead speaker announced the final boarding call for Bora Bora.

I pointed to the ceiling. "That's us."

Laughing, we sprinted to our terminal, sliding through the doors just before they were being closed.

CHAPTER FORTY

Trevor

I LOOKED around the little hut we'd be staying in for the next week. "Please tell me this didn't cost you ten-thousand dollars," I finally said. It was beautiful, but...

I propped the large rolling suitcase against the wall. Callie assured me that she packed things for me too; that all our things were in this suitcase.

I knew how Callie packed. I'd seen it with my own eyes, her putting her entire closet in a suitcase for a weekend getaway.

This suitcase wasn't very big, which meant there was a very real possibility that there weren't very many clothes in that thing...

The thought excited me.

Callie walked around the room before settling on the bed, shaking her head. "No. I got it for a steal. A good deal. Because you're worth a little more than a one-K exotic vacay." She said the words sassily, but at the same time, I could hear the hurt and regret in her words.

I moved to sit on the bed beside her, but quickly, Callie pushed me down, only to cuddle into my chest. Easily, I wrapped an arm around her shoulders as she propped her chin on me.

"I can't cancel New York," she said, completely killing the mood.

I nodded, staying quiet. I hated the thought that we had this two weeks, and then who knew what the hell would happen. I meant it when I told her I didn't want to hold her back. I wanted for her what *she* wanted for her, and if that meant I had to let her go in the process...

"But I can put in my resignation with the company for when the assignment is up. I'd be doing it for me, so don't even start with that argument," she said, as if she knew I'd somehow fight her on it.

My girl knew me well.

Although, I didn't think she had to give up nursing.

"I love you, Trevor," she continued, her voice soft once again. "We've both made some pretty stupid decisions in the heat of the moment, but I know that at the end of the day, you always have my back. And I want to always have yours. It's just four months. And then when I come home, it will be for good. I'll go wherever you go. I like to travel, but I love being with you so much more."

And then she sealed the deal with her lips on mine.

We didn't come up for air for an hour.

Then, after a quick walk on the beach, it was another five before we made it back outside.

This was heaven. Not being in Bora Bora, although it was nice.

No. Heaven was loving Callie.

I didn't plan on letting her go again.

I'd fight till the end, convincing her I was the one for her.

That we were meant to be together.

Because when it came to Callie and me? I refused to lose.

EPILOGUE

December 20

Trevor

I SAT NEAR BAGGAGE CLAIM, anxious to see her.

Four months was a fucking long time, and the single game we had out in New York, wasn't nearly enough.

We'd perfected the art of phone and video sex but *damn*, I needed my hands on her flesh. I needed to hold her, to kiss her...

The baggage carousel began to turn, and I stood anxiously, looking toward the escalator for the coming travelers,

Any moment now, I'd see her.

I'd hold her...

I'd have to get my feels in now, though, because we were due to a team Christmas gathering in two hours.

Not nearly enough time to do everything I wanted to do to her. With her.

People began to appear, coming down the escalators in,

at first, groups of two and three, then larger groups. I looked over the heads, trying to spot her blonde hair. Every time I thought I saw her, I was disappointed when the woman got to the base of the escalator and people moved, showing she was not, indeed, my Callie.

My eyes were traveling up and down the moving stairs, hoping to see her...

Then a hand was in the air.

I didn't even need to see her face to know it was her. My grin was widespread before I even saw her face.

I made my way toward her, walking against foot traffic to reach her.

Callie's smile was as big as mine as she moved away from the escalator.

"My God, look at you," I told my wife as she came close, my hands automatically moving to her belly. I fell to my knees, resting my forehead against the tiny swell of her stomach.

Callie's hands were in my hair and when I looked up at her, she had tears in her eyes, just as I had them in mine.

I stood, taking her face then, and kissing her softly.

Our week in Bora Bora ended with a marriage, and, unbeknownst to us at the time, a pregnancy. The marriage was talked about in-depth before we actually went through with it on the day before returning to San Diego.

The pregnancy?

Shit. I could still remember, with amazing clarity, the feeling of dread I had in the pit of my stomach when I turned on my phone after a game, and the only message was one from Callie. *Call me as soon as you get home. I don't care how late it is.*

I didn't bother with a phone call.

I didn't even bother driving home.

I video-called her while sitting in my truck, in the

Enforcers' garage. I was terrified something happened to her, and I couldn't do anything to help her, not while I was on the west coast and she was way on the east.

Obviously, I knew if I had to get out to her, I'd be able to. It would happen.

When she opened the video line, her face was red and blotchy. She yelled at me for not calling, and I asked, again and again, what was wrong. What I could do to help.

Then she showed me the pregnancy test, saying she must have forgotten her birth control when we'd been apart and fighting. I heard none of it. Rather, I didn't care about it.

That moment was the very best of my life.

Waiting two more months to see her? Not my best moments. The team's schedule didn't leave much room to do extra travel to New York to see her, and she had to work over Thanksgiving, so there went that small break in time.

The first four months of our marriage were reduced to phone calls and video chats, but that was now all in the past.

"God, I love you," I finally told her, to her face, after all this time apart.

Never again. No more distance.

Her smile softened, but her love for me shone bright in her eyes. "I love you too. Now, let's get my things and go to the party. The sooner we do, the sooner you can bring me home."

Home.

I couldn't freaking wait.

BONUS EPILOGUE
CALLIE

August 8
Seventeen Years Later

I was proud of myself, I thought as I stood in the doorway of our foyer, watching as Trevor laughed, pushing Caleb Prescott off the patio.

It had been a few years since our families had gotten together, with Caleb coaching in San Diego and Trevor coaching college hockey in Madison, Wisconsin. In the summers, Trevor and our family made our way back to San Diego, but Caleb and *his* family were taking that time to come to Wisconsin.

Trevor and Caleb were still good friends, as were Sydney and I—we were far closer than I would have ever thought in those first years—but life didn't allow us to do a lot together.

So, when Trevor's fiftieth birthday had been coming up...

I decided to surprise him with the Prescotts coming to town.

With Caleb and Sydney Prescott now gone, Trevor

came back into the house, locking the front door before turning toward me, his brows raised into his sparsely-speckled hair. "You," he said, stalking toward me.

"You," I repeated, my arms crossed and my own brows lifted.

"I said no birthday shit."

I smiled wide at him as he neared. "When have I ever listened to you?"

"Never," he admitted, wrapping an arm around me while his other went to my hair, fisting it in his hand to pull my head back. He stared down at me for a good four seconds before lowering his mouth to mine.

"Gross!" came from somewhere in the vicinity behind us, and rather than lift his face from mine, Trevor merely laughed against my lips, kissing twice more before looking behind me.

"Why aren't you in bed?" he asked our youngest. At twelve, Kendall was proving to be her father's largest heartache. He'd been good with boys, but the moment the sonographer said, "It's a girl..." he was a goner.

"I wanted to sneak ice cream cake," she answered, raising her chin.

Have two stubborn people procreate...

And the result was staring back at us.

Hey, at least she was honest.

Our other two were stubborn, yes, but Kennedy brought out a whole new game.

I turned in my husband's arms, even though he didn't let go of me. Leaning back into Trevor's chest, I informed our daughter, "I found six glasses in your room. Six, Kenny. No more food in your room." She was a dish hoarder, it would appear.

"But mom..."

"Listen to your mother." Trevor was generally a

pushover when it came to our kids, but he knew when to stand behind my decisions, making us a pretty good tag team.

"Fine," she mumbled, turning away and stomping—as if she weighed two-hundred pounds, unlike the eighty-five that she did—to her room.

"Don't wake up your brother!" Trevor called out.

Colton was typically a heavy sleeper, but he was particularly sensitive to any noises his sister made. I loved that, even at fifteen and in that stage where he hated everyone, he was so protective over her.

Unlike their oldest brother…

"Shouldn't Dylan be home?" Trevor asked, letting go of me to walk toward the garage door, where he *knew* our son's car was *not*.

"I told him to be home by midnight." I walked into the kitchen to begin cleaning up. It wasn't that Dylan wasn't protective of Kendall, because if something happened to her, he'd be the first in line to fix the problem.

But our oldest was more than ready to flee the coop.

Too bad he had another year, I thought with a well-intended snigger.

"Who's he with tonight?" Trevor came in, helping me. I may have been a stay-at-home mom for the better part of seventeen years, but Trevor never expected the house things to fall all on my shoulders. Just like raising our kids, we made a pretty good team all-around.

"Brooks." Knowing our oldest was hanging out with one of the Prescott boys seemed to appease him. The youngest Prescott kids all stayed back at a nearby hotel while Caleb and Sydney came here to celebrate Trevor's trek down the other side of the hill.

So, with a grin, I decided to add, "But really, you know he's hanging out with Brae."

His hands stilled over the pan of appetizers he was covering, so I continued to taunt him. "I give it five years before you're knocking back whiskey with Caleb, at a wedding."

"If he knocks her up..."

I laughed loudly, my head falling back. After I was through, I shook my head, "Why does your head automatically go to sex? Besides, they're only sixteen."

"I know my boy. He's no saint." Trevor shook his head. "Shit, Caleb will kill me if something happens to his daughter. Gotta have the talk with Dyl. Fuck."

I laughed again. "Trevor, it's too late for the birds and the bees. That ship has sailed."

"What do you know of it?" His eyes were wide.

"I make it a habit to clean our children's rooms at least once a week. Dylan's been hoarding condoms for a year." Knowing your sixteen-year-old was having sex, didn't do great things to a mom's heart, but, "I figured you'd talked to him about sex." And knowing my husband and, yeah, his 'rules,' I knew he'd have taught our son well.

If Dylan was having sex, then he was doing it with a good head on his shoulders.

Hopefully.

"Yeah, once. But I didn't realize I needed to add, *and these are the girls you never look twice at.*"

"God, you're funny," I blurted, food forgotten as I walked to my husband.

Eighteen years since the day we met, and he was still making me laugh, making me smile.

"You don't understand," Trevor continued, shaking his head even though my arms were wrapping around him. "Brae is his baby. Caleb will not stop at a shotgun if anything happens to her."

I grinned up at him. "I know." Before I could say

anything else though, the door to the garage opened, and the rumble of the actual garage door closing, filled the room.

Trevor looked over his shoulder at our oldest.

A few inches taller than his dad, he was a good mix of both of us, with Trevor's dark hair and my blue eyes. Those very eyes landed on us.

"Your room," Trevor said over his shoulder.

"Trevor..."

"Dad."

"There are some girls you don't look twice at," Trevor informed him. "Braelyn Prescott is one of them."

"I didn't..." Dylan's eyes cut to me, and his face scowled comically. "Mom."

I just smiled wide. "Sorry, bud. You're going to have to work on that one on your own."

...Because I knew things his father didn't. Things that involved a fairly involved long-distance relationship.

Dylan grumbled as he walked past.

"Love you," Trevor called out, before whispering down to me, "I said it first."

I rolled my eyes, whispering back, "It's not a race." Then, I called out as well, "Love you, Dylan."

Our son grumbled his goodnights and it wasn't much longer before the kitchen was cleaned, and the house closed up, with my husband and I in our room, settled for the night.

With his big body between my legs, his hips pushing as he thrust into me slowly, and my hands locked above my head, held by one of his own, Trevor whispered promises of love in my ear.

Who would have thought eighteen years ago, that a ride home would lead to all of this?

I certainly couldn't have imagined it.

Besides, it was so much better than I would have ever fathomed.

Life with Trevor was worth the ups and downs.

So, so worth them all.

The next Enforcer to fall? None other than a certain Mikey Leeds.
This young widower learns that sometimes forever's always been in front of you...

25: Angels and Assists is now available!

A QUICK LOOK AT 25: ANGELS AND ASSITS

CAMEOS

Who did you meet in 32: *Refuse to Lose* who has a book?
Let's see...

Caleb & Sydney Prescott — Interference
Porter Prescott — The Playmaker
Jonny Prescott — Butterfly Save
Mikey Leeds — 25: Angels and Assists

Other books to keep your eyes open for include:
Carter Douglas in *Desired*
Nico D'Amaco in 82: *Coast to Coast*

25: ANGELS AND ASSISTS PREVIEW

Euphoria.

That's what this was.

The rush, the adrenaline.

And with a team that took a mid-season risk on me.

Me.

A kid from nowhere-Nebraska.

Sure, on paper, I was a semi-good bet. I played hard. Fought harder. I didn't have the support at home, with a dad who could give two shits what his sixteen-year-old did in his "spare" time—and by "spare," I meant the time I hadn't been working at the local grocery store, to help pay bills... and to support his beer habit.

But I never let the lack of someone in my corner, deter me from being the best player I could be.

Eighteen.

The first year that my life was set to change.

A month after my eighteenth birthday, I was drafted by Quebec. *Fucking drafted*! Talk about elation. A kid who played club-hockey, and an NHL team was interested in him. I didn't play for Quebec the first two seasons, not after an evaluation period, but it didn't make a difference. I gave up my right to play in college with the NCAA, and played semi-professionally with Quebec's Ontario Hockey League team, a Junior hockey league.

I did all of it in hopes that maybe my dad would appreciate me, cheer for me...shit, maybe even just give a damn about me.

No such luck.

I didn't talk to my dad anymore, but the draft and OHL had been my ticket to a better life. It was in Canada that I met my wife.

The Gagnons, my host family, were close to the Perri family, and even though I was working on playing professionally and Trina Perri was finishing up her final year in high school—*secondary school, excuse me*—it was easy to fall for the pretty blonde with a slight French accent.

We were married sixteen months after meeting, only four months after her seventeenth birthday.

A few months after that, I earned my spot on the Quebec roster.

Life was fucking glorious.

For three seconds, anyway.

I didn't see a lick of NHL playing time. Sure, a few minutes every few games, but that's not what a guy looked for when it came time to play in the Show.

Times at home were starting to get stressful. Two young kids, on their own, newly married. Needless to say, the honeymoon period ended fast.

Ended even faster with the realization that we were expecting a baby.

Trina wasn't working. I wasn't actually playing. I never thought that I'd have to be a penny-pincher, not if I had an NHL contract, but when you weren't playing the minutes you wanted, and you didn't know if you were going to be resigned, and you didn't have a non-hockey playing career to fall back on...

You pinched those pennies.

Anderson was born on a sunny day in May, to parents who were hardly more than babies themselves, at all of twenty-one, and a month shy of nineteen.

I was re-signed just two weeks later.

Life seemed good; I had a new three-year contract, a little more per year than the previous years. Enough to keep us more than comfortable if, heaven forbid, something happened, and I couldn't play.

We hadn't been expecting the call downs and the call backs and the waivers. *So many damn times, this last year and a half.* Due to an oversight on Quebec's part, I played too many NHL games before being sent back to my OHL team, and thus, my professional career had begun during my first contract —marking *this* year as the year waivers kicked in for me. In layman's terms, waivers meant that any other team could grab you and take over your contract, while you were going between your contracted team's AHL and NHL teams. If you were a nobody, you were generally safe to return to your team.

If I'd been just *any* kid, I didn't think waivers were such a big deal. It sucked, yeah, to be called up and sent down; not knowing if you were playing, or when you were playing, or, shit, *where* you were playing.

But here I was—newly married, with a new baby, and I had to leave Trina in Quebec while I went wherever the hell the higher ups wanted me to go—which had been St. Paul, Minnesota. This last season, though, we got smart; we rented a condo in St. Paul so we could be together during my lengthy call-downs.

Two weeks ago, though, on my way back up on the ladder of hockey, I got the news.

I was picked up on waivers.

Now, some guys hated those words just as much as the word 'trade', but if it meant I was going to start *playing*, shit, I was all about it—and San Diego held promise. They liked my playing style, and wanted to help mold me into a bigger, better player.

And they wanted my wife, son, and me to "get comfortable."

Trina and I splurged, finding ourselves a tiny oceanside condo, rather than a rental, just outside San Diego. Cute. Little. A mortgage that wasn't going to break the bank, and one I could make work if something were to happen to my career.

The last two weeks, even though a whirlwind, made the last years seem like a bad dream.

Every home game this week, Trina and Anderson had been up in the seats, cheering the team on. They watched as I had my first major, consistent ice time—I played no less than nine minutes a game, which was a huge difference from Quebec. I had a couple hits, some note-worthy play-making times, and even an assist.

They weren't here tonight though, and I was disappointed that I'd made my first professional goal when they weren't witness to it. With Christmas just two days away, Trina and Anderson flew back to Quebec a few nights before, and I'd join them in the morning.

...and I was going to bug the shit out of her with YouTube videos, the moment I had my wife in my arms again.

"You fucking did it!" Trevor Winksi yelled, standing up as I skated toward the bench, my gloved fist out as I prepared to go down the bench for customary post-goal fist bumps. I found a mentor in team assistant captain Trevor

Winski, and it was, no doubt, because of him and his patience, that it was *me* who just lit that red light.

"Way to fucking go, kid!" he yelled again when I stepped into the bench, a grin stretched across my face. Winski grabbed my padded shoulders and shook me around. "Knew you fucking could."

I was only six years younger than him, but I didn't mind being called *kid*, not when I had a tough-as-shit player being my team BFF. He was buddy-buddy with our captain, Caleb Prescott, and therefore, with the team's goaltender, Jonny Prescott, too. 'Prescott' ran hockey here in San Diego, and I had to admit—being accepted into the personal fold, even if it was through Winski, was a pretty big accomplishment.

I didn't imagine that being Winski's friend was going to be the deciding factor on if I was staying here or shipping to Beloit, the farm team for the Enforcers club, but I didn't think it hurt to be close to those guys.

I laughed, back in the moment, as I pulled my glove off and reached for a water bottle. "It was fucking beautiful, wasn't it?"

He elbowed me as I brought the pop-top bottle to my mouth, nodding up at the Jumbotron. "I don't know, kid; you tell me."

Tilting my head back, I watched the replay, finally focusing in on the fact the arena was still yelling out cheers. Some classic rock song was blaring on the speakers, but my attention was firmly on the Jumbotron.

Hard battle in the corner. I got the puck out, but lost it. Jordan Byrd managed possession, clearing it to the other side of the zone. Bodies moved around the ice; the boards and Plexiglas rattled when players were thrown into it.

Suddenly, the puck landed by my feet.

Quick thinking. That's what the moment was.

Quick, on your feet, thinking.

I pushed the puck around the back of the net, slipping it in on the other side, just between the goalie's skate and post...

The play happened in seconds, but remembering it...

It was in slow-motion.

The type of slow-motion that had you excited and waiting for more.

I was going to remember this game for the rest of my fucking life.

———

"Leeds, back with me," John Mitchem, the team's equipment manager, said, as he reached for my elbow. We'd just walked off the bench, the team heading to the locker rooms between periods.

Two down, one to go.

"Yeah, sure," I replied, pulling off my helmet as I lumbered on my skates, behind him. I couldn't imagine what he needed me for, but I racked my brain anyway.

I didn't break a stick, and skates were moving fine.

I glanced down at my shoulder; maybe there was a snag or rip that needed to be mended from a hit I took against the boards.

Nothing.

Huh.

John walked me past the locker room, just a bit further down the hall. From here, you could still hear the excited echo of fans up above. The atmosphere was ridiculous.

It was easy to feel a high, when you played with a team with fans like San Diego's.

"What's up, John?" I asked, glancing over my shoulder as the last of the guys headed into the locker room. I wasn't sure why we'd stopped here, and not in the locker room, or, hell, even in the training room. Why in the hall?

"You need to shower and dress."

My frown was automatic. "What do you mean, I have to shower and dress?" I'd been doing well. Where the hell would the team be sending me, the day before break? Why would I be leaving in the middle of a game? Why—

"There was an accident."

The moment the plane's wheels touched down at Quebec City Jean Lesage, I turned my phone off airplane mode. I hadn't stopped bouncing my knee the entire flight; hadn't slept a damn wink, either. I needed to be in Quebec, and not in San Diego; I needed to be in communication with the Perris.

Spending half a fucking day on a commercial flight did not allow for that it. Hell, the four-hour layover in New York was enough to have me crawling through the walls.

No one was telling me anything. Nothing of importance, anyway.

Everyone was being vague, just saying *get to the hospital. You just need to get to the hospital.*

The stress of the unknown had me not taking their calls. Not while I was in New York, where I couldn't do anything. There weren't any earlier connections; I asked no less than five times, to five different attendants.

The seatbelt lights were hardly off, and I was unbuckled and standing from my first-class seat, antsy to get off this fucking metal bird.

I needed to get off...

I needed—

My phone pinged, announcing messages, now that my

data was turned back on. I glanced at the screen, taking in the quick influx of names:

Trina's parents.

Luc Gagnon, the man who was more a father to me than my own had ever been.

Sam, his son, and therefore, my pseudo-brother.

Molly.

I swallowed hard at seeing Anderson's nanny's name on my screen. Hell, 'nanny' was just the term we used for her when it came to my accountant.

Molly was Trina's friend.

One of her only friends in the states.

Truly *only* unless you counted the hockey wives and girlfriends she'd gotten to know in the last year.

Trina and Molly met when I was playing in Minnesota, right before Anderson was born. When my wife brought up hiring Molly as a nanny, I was put-off by it. Not because I didn't like the girl, but because we didn't *need* a nanny. Trina was home, and it wasn't like I was gone *all* of the time. But, when Molly came out for an informal interview, I realized that it wasn't so much a nanny that Trina wanted, but a close friend who was around—and *that* I could support.

I had an entire locker room of guys I could befriend. Trina had no one, *knew* no one, other than me. She was in a new country with a new husband and a new baby...

The least I could do was let her find a girlfriend.

So, at the laughing expense of my wife, I moved money around in our budget, so I would feel comfortable 'affording' her, and contacted our accountant. The next day, Anderson was born.

Molly was as much a part of his life, as Trina and I were.

Because Trina and Molly were damn near connected at the hip, she went up to Quebec with Trina and Anderson for Christmas. I wasn't sure why she didn't go home to her own family, but again, it made Trina happy, so I was for it.

Now, though...

My thumb hovered over Molly's name. She'd tried to get ahold of me the most times, and because of that, I was absolutely terrified of what she was going to say.

All that I'd been told before leaving San Diego, was that Trina and Anderson had been in a car accident, and that I needed to get to Quebec.

Now, I stood, nervous energy coursing through me, as I pleaded in my head for the attendants to open the door. As soon as it was, I was off the plane and rushing through the airport, thankful for my permanent resident card. My messages were the last thing on my mind. I didn't want to see them.

I didn't want confirmation of my fears.

I couldn't...

Fuck. I couldn't live with myself if I knew something bad had happened to either of them.

They're fine. They're fine. They're fine.

In my hand, my cell began to vibrate with an incoming call. As I rushed through the people, I opened the call, not bothering to look at who it was from.

It could only be from Trina's parents, the Gagnons, or Molly.

"Mikey." Molly's voice came out in a whoosh.

My steps faltered, but I pushed on. "How are they? Tell me they're okay, Molly. Tell me..." I swallowed hard, looking to my left, my right, then heading down the left hallway. My dress shoes clicked against the polished floors, slipping in some spots.

"I've got the car in the pick-up line, right outside," she said, avoiding my questions.

"Molly." My blood was roaring through my ears.

229

"Molly, just tell me." The feeling in my gut was horrible. Something was terribly wrong.

Why wasn't she telling me anything?

"We have to get to the hospital," she managed, and I could hear the slightest of cracks in her voice. "Please, just hurry." Then she hung up on me.

Molly hung up on me.

Growling my frustration, I pocketed my phone in my sport jacket and tried to focus on the anger, the unknowing...

But when I got through the sliding doors and the cold winter air hit my face, when Molly's face came to view...

I just knew.

"No." One word. The only word to pass my lips the moment I saw Trina's only friend. Molly's normally young, jovial face—the one that made her look more like fifteen than twenty—was ashen, her eyes puffy, her brown hair falling out of a badly placed ponytail. I stopped in my spot, still easily fifteen feet between us. "No. They're fine. Molly, tell me they're fine." I could not be a twenty-two-year-old widow, who lost both his wife and his son. I couldn't be.

A sob broke from her lips as she lifted a woolen mitten to her mouth, her eyes filling with tears.

"Molly, tell me!"

My feet were glued to the concrete.

I couldn't move if I tried.

For the second time in twelve hours, my world began to move in slow-motion. The sounds of cars moving and loading, planes taking off, people chatting, a solitaire bell being rung outside the small airport...it all faded out. All I saw, all I could fixate on, was Molly's face as her shoulders folded in, tears falling from her eyes, and her head...

Shaking no.

FINAL WORDS FROM MIGNON

Let me tell you a little bit about Trevor Winski.

...he was never supposed to have a story.

I knew when he first smiled at Sydney in *Interference* that he was a good friend of Caleb's. I knew he was close with the Prescott family, when he teased Porter at the end of *The Playmaker*. But it wasn't until he told Marlo that he had a date (in the currently unavailable *27: Dropping the Gloves*), and with *whom*...that I realized the man was just sitting on the sidelines, patiently biding his time until he told me: Change your plans; I'm next.

...next, let me tell you about Callie. Have you been keeping up with the Prescotts and Jenna's hold on Jonny? Were you surprised that Jenna had a sister? ME TOO!!!!

You may hear authors saying they're "pantsers" vs "plotters." What that means is, regardless of the characters speaking to the author, because we all swear we're not crazy even though people 'talk' to us in our heads, it comes down to how the story presents itself. Some authors plan every last detail of a story. They're plotters. Others, like myself, just let the characters take control. We write by the seat of our pants.

I'm often curious how a story would have ended up if I'd written more or less on any given day. The Playmaker is *nothing* like the story that I first had in my head eight years ago, because I let Porter and Asher (let's be honest...it was all Porter) drive that story. It was supposed to be enemies-to-lovers, and if you've read the duet, you know that Porter laid claim on Asher the moment she crossed his path.

So, I was just as shocked as my readers when I found out Jenna had a sister. I could have fought it, but the last time I tried to fight what the characters were telling me, I suffered a two-week-long writer's block (*All Night Long*, Rory and Emily).

Nobody likes Jenna, so I knew that if Trevor was going to fall for her sister—if he was introduced to her through the Prescotts—the sister had to be something special.

I absolutely enjoyed writing Trevor and Callie's story. It, like *The Playmaker*, took some turns I wasn't planning for but I hope that you enjoyed their story as they wanted it to be told.

Thank you to my PA, Melissa, for being quite the cheerleader—even during those times that she scolded me for leaving her hanging, while having her read as I was writing. I left her in quite uncomfortable positions...and maybe had her cry once, too.

To my editor, Jenn. Thank you for helping make my babies shine. I appreciate you more than you could ever know, and I can only hope that someday, our partnership will shine brighter and further than I could imagine.

Melissa and Jenn together...those two keep me on my toes. I've enjoyed our conversations, ladies.

To my early ARC readers. Your guys' reactions to this story had me grinning from ear to ear on more than one occasion—especially during a week that I needed smiles.

You see, ten days before publication, I had to let go of

my cat. I know, I know, she's just a cat. During a time that so many other *nasty* things are going on in our world—wildfires, Harvey, Irma—what's the loss of a cat? There will be readers who read this, and completely understand. She (and her littermate, who I had to put down nearly two years ago) were my first responsibilities as an adult. Losing her was hard. She sat beside me during the last twenty-thousand words of this story.

Anyway.

Finally, to my readers. I can't believe that I've been publishing for sixteen months, and the group of you keeps GROWING. Never in my wildest dreams could I fathom that more than a handful of people would read my books, and LIKE them.

Thank you, thank you, thank you.

ABOUT THE AUTHOR

Mignon Mykel is the author of the Prescott Family series, as well as the short-novella romance series, O'Gallagher Nights. When not sitting at Starbucks writing whatever her characters tell her to, you can find her hiking in the mountains of her new home in Arizona, or trying to tame her sassy (see: stubborn) mastiff-lab.

For early access and exclusive behind the scenes access, be sure to find her on Patreon!